MRS. PIGGLE-WIGGLE

Mrs. Piggle-Wiggle

Betty MacDonald

Pictures by HILARY KNIGHT

HarperTrophy®
A Division of HarperCollins*Publishers*

Mrs. Piggle-Wiggle
Text copyright 1947 by Betty MacDonald
Text copyright renewed 1975 by Donald C. MacDonald
Illustrations copyright © 1957 by J.B. Lippincott Company
Illustrations copyright renewed 1985 by Hilary Knight
Library of Congress Catalog Card Number: 85-43013
ISBN 0-397-31712-3
ISBN 0-06-440148-0 (pbk.)
First Harper Trophy edition, 1985.

For Anne, Joan, Mari, Salli Heidi,
Darsie, Frankie and Stevie

who are perfect angels and couldn't
possibly have been the inspiration for
any of these stories.

Contents

1

MRS. PIGGLE-WIGGLE, HERSELF

I expect I might as well begin by telling you all about Mrs. Piggle-Wiggle so that whenever I mention her name, which I do very often in this book, you will not interrupt and ask, "Who is Mrs. Piggle-Wiggle? What does she look like? How big is she? How old is she? What color is her hair? Is her hair long? Does she wear high heels? Does she have any children? Is there a Mr. Piggle-Wiggle?"

Mrs. Piggle-Wiggle lives here in our town. She is very small and has a hump on her back. When children ask her about the hump, she says, "Oh that's a big lump of magic.

Sometimes it turns me into a witch; other times into a dwarf or a fairy, and on special occasions it makes me into a queen." The children are all very envious of the hump because, besides being magic, it is such a convenient fastening place for wings.

Mrs. Piggle-Wiggle has brown sparkly eyes and brown hair which she keeps very long, almost to her knees, so the children can comb it. She usually wears it on top of her head in a knot, unless someone has been combing it and then she has braids, or long wet curls, or long hair just hanging and with a jewelled crown or flowers on top.

One day I saw her digging in her garden wearing the jewelled crown and with her hair billowing down her back. She waved gaily and said, "I promised Betsy (Betsy is one of her children friends) that I would not touch this hair until she came home from school," and she went on with her digging. Mrs. Piggle-Wiggle's skin is a goldy brown and she has a warm, spicy, sugar-cooky smell that is very comforting to children who are sad about something. Her clothes are all brown and never look crisp and pressed because they are used for dress-up. She wears felt hats which the children poke and twist into witches' and pirates' hats and she does not mind at all. Sunday mornings she takes one of the hats off the closet shelf, gives it a few thumps, pulls it firmly down fore and aft and wears it to church. She wears very high heels all the time and is glad to let the little girls borrow her shoes.

Mrs. Piggle-Wiggle has no family at all. She says that her husband, Mr. Piggle-Wiggle, was a pirate and after he had buried all of his treasure in the back yard, he died. She just has herself and Wag, her dog, and Lightfoot, her cat.

The most remarkable thing about Mrs. Piggle-Wiggle is her house, which is upside down. It is a little brown house, and sitting there in its tangly garden it looks like a small brown puppy lying on its back with its feet in the air. Mrs. Piggle-Wiggle says that when she was a little girl she used to lie in bed and gaze up at the ceiling and wonder and wonder what it would be like if the house were upside down. And so when she grew up and built her own house she had it built upside down, just to see. The bathroom, the kitchen and the staircase are right side up—they are more convenient that way. You can easily see that you could not cook on an upside-down stove or wash dishes in an upside-down sink or walk *up* upside-down stairs.

In the living room of her house is a large chandelier and instead of being on the ceiling it is on the floor. Of course it is really on the ceiling, but the ceiling is the floor and so it is on the floor and the children turn on the lights and then squat around it pretending it is a campfire. Mrs. Piggle-Wiggle says that her chandelier is the only one in town which is put to any real use. Her bedrooms all have slidy boards in them because if you will look up at your attic ceiling you will see that a slanty ceiling when turned upside

11

down makes a fine slidy board. Also all the wall lights are very close to the floor and handy for the small children. For the first five or ten years after the house was built Mrs. Piggle-Wiggle climbed in and out of her rooms over the high doorways but now she has little steps which are just the thing to practise jumping. She gives the children chalk so they can mark on the rug how far they jump.

Nobody knows how old Mrs. Piggle-Wiggle is. She says she doesn't know herself. She says, "What difference does it make how old I am when I shall never grow any bigger."

Mrs. Piggle-Wiggle's dog, Wag, has puppies every once in a while and so she keeps a long list of names of children who want them on the blackboard in her kitchen. For Lightfoot-the-cat's kittens she has a long waiting list on the blackboard in the dining room.

Mrs. Piggle-Wiggle's back yard is full of big holes where small boys dig for Mr. Piggle-Wiggle's buried treasure and her front yard is full of flowers which the little girls pick, jam into vases and place about her living room or carry to their teachers.

Every child in town is a friend of Mrs. Piggle-Wiggle's but she knows very few of their parents. She says grown-ups make her nervous.

For the first year after she built her house, Mrs. Piggle-Wiggle lived there all by herself except for Wag and Lightfoot, and she was very lonely. Then, one dark, rainy afternoon when she was baking sugar cookies and thinking how much fun it would be if she knew someone besides Wag and Lightfoot to invite for tea, she happened to look out of her kitchen window and there coming up the street in the pouring rain, dragging a big suitcase and bawling, was a little girl. Mrs. Piggle-Wiggle wiped the flour off her hands and hurried right out into the rain and invited the little girl in for tea.

The little girl's name was Mary Lou Robertson and she was eight years old and quite fat, and she was running away from home. She told Mrs. Piggle-Wiggle all this after she had drunk three cups of cambric tea and eaten seven sugar cookies. She said, "I'm running away from home because I hate to wash dishes. All I do is wash dishes. I am just a servant. Dishes! Dishes! Dishes! Wash, dry, put away. That's all I do. My mother doesn't love me at all. She isn't my real mother, anyway. She probably got me out of an orphanage just to wash her dishes." Mary Lou began to cry again, so that the eighth sugar cooky got quite soggy before she finished it.

Mrs. Piggle-Wiggle said, "Isn't she your real mother?"

Mary Lou said, "She says she is but no real mother would make you wash dishes. Wash dishes! Wash dishes!"

"Now that's a funny thing," said Mrs. Piggle-Wiggle. "I mean your hating to wash dishes so much, because you see, I like to wash dishes. In fact I enjoy washing dishes so much that a cause of great sorrow to me is the fact that the only dishes I must wash are for Wag, Lightfoot and me. Three or four dishes a meal, that is all.

"When I wash dishes, Mary Lou, I pretend that I am a beautiful princess with long, golden, curly hair (Mary Lou's hair was jet black and braided into two stiff little pigtails), and apple-blossom skin and forget-me-not blue eyes. I have been captured by a wicked witch and my only chance to get free is to wash every single dish and have the whole kitchen sparkly clean before the clock strikes. For, when the clock strikes, the witch will come down and inspect, to see if there is a crumb anywhere. If there are pots and pans that have been put away wet, if the silverware has been thrown in the drawer, or if the sink has not been scrubbed out, the witch will have me in her power for another year."

Mrs. Piggle-Wiggle looked at the clock and jumped up. "It is ten minutes to four, Princess, and we have so much to do. Hurry, hurry, hurry!" Mary Lou also jumped up and began carrying the tea things to the sink and Mrs. Piggle-Wiggle whisked them in and out of the dish water and Mary Lou dried them and Mrs. Piggle-Wiggle hurried as fast as she could and put the cooky things away and every once in a while she would stop and say, "Hark, Princess, do you hear the thump of the witch's big gnarly cane?" Then Mary Lou, her braids bobbing up and down with excitement, would say, "I hear it, Princess, it is coming closer and closer." Soon the kitchen sparkled, the dishes

14

were washed and dried and put away and every crumb had been swept off the floor. Mary Lou even curled Light-foot's tail neatly around her legs and smoothed Wag's fur. Just before the clock struck, Mrs. Piggle-Wiggle said to Mary Lou, "Princess, I must leave you now but show the witch your work and oh, I do hope you will be freed!"

Then she went upstairs and pretty soon down the stairs came a terrible old witch with a long black dress, a tall black hat and a big gnarly black cane. Mary Lou was very scared until she saw the sparkly eyes of Mrs. Piggle-Wiggle under the black hat. She showed the witch the kitchen and the witch took out the cooky pans and carried them over to the light to see if they were clean and dry. She got down on her knees, squeaking like a rusty gate, to see if Mary Lou had swept under the stove. She felt inside the teacups to see if there was sugar in the bottoms and she put on her glasses to examine the sink. But she could not find anything wrong so she handed Mary Lou the key to the kitchen door and screeched out, "You are free, Princess, but I will get you again, never fear!" The witch clumped back up the stairs and in a few minutes down came Mrs. Piggle-Wiggle.

"Well," said Mrs. Piggle-Wiggle, "do you see why I like to wash dishes?"

Mary Lou said, "Oh, Mrs. Piggle-Wiggle that was the most fun I've ever had!"

Mrs. Piggle-Wiggle said, "Of course you can have more fun than I can because you have so many more dishes to wash. If I only had more dishes and could take longer I would be a princess with curly, yellow, long hair, apple-blossom skin, blue eyes and a beautiful voice and I would sing sad songs over the dishpan. Also if I had more dishes I would have the witch ride through the night on a broom-stick and I would creep out on the back porch to see if she was coming. I could hear her land with a thump on the roof and I would slip upstairs to see if she was going to slide down the chimney or thump down the stairs. Oh, there would be ever so many exciting things to pretend if only I had more dishes to wash."

After a while it stopped raining and the sun came out and Mary Lou took her suitcase and went home. That night her mother (it really was her mother, of course) almost fainted when she came out to the kitchen exactly twenty-seven minutes after dinner and Mary Lou was sweeping the floor and all the dishes were washed and dried and put away and everything was immaculate. Mrs. Robertson rushed in and called Mary Lou's father and he came out to the kitchen and pretended to fall on the floor with surprise and then he said to Mary Lou's mother, "I like your new maid, madam. In fact, she is so much better than Tillie Slopwash who used to be here that I think we should invite her to the moving picture show some early evening."

Then Mary Lou told them all about Mrs. Piggle-Wiggle and Mary Lou's mother said, "Oh, yes, I remember seeing that odd little house. She sounds like a charming friend and if you are certain that she invited you, you may go over there after school tomorrow."

The next day after school Mary Lou went to see Mrs. Piggle-Wiggle. She took her best friend, Kitty Wheeling, with her, and Mrs. Piggle-Wiggle was very glad to see them and showed them through her upside-down house and served tea and cookies. Kitty said, her mouth full of cooky, "My worst trouble is bedmaking. I just cannot get them smooth. I'd much rather wash dishes like Mary Lou, but Mother won't let me change with my sister, Sally, who washes the dishes, until I have learned to make beds properly. Oh, I just despise to make beds!"

Mrs. Piggle-Wiggle poured herself another cup of tea, gave a saucer of cream to Lightfoot and four cookies to Wag, then said, "If you think you have a hard time making beds, Kitty, imagine how hard it is for me. You see, the Cruel Queen sleeps in my beds every night and inspects them every morning and if *she* finds a single wrinkle, even one as big as a pin, she will have me thrown in a dungeon. Come upstairs and I'll show you how I have to make beds."

They went upstairs and Mrs. Piggle-Wiggle threw the covers clear off the foot of one of her own beds, then she had Kitty help her make it and when they finished it was as smooth as the floor—no wrinkles. Mrs. Piggle-Wiggle said, "The secret is to throw the covers way back. You simply cannot smooth up a bed because if you do there might be a wrinkle down by the foot and of course the

Cruel Queen will find it and then DOWN INTO THE DUNGEON!"

Mrs. Piggle-Wiggle took the bed all apart again and said, "Now, Kitty, you and Mary Lou make the bed while I tell the Cruel Queen you are ready for inspection." She went into the closet and shut the door. When she came out just as Kitty and Mary Lou finished the bed, she was no longer Mrs. Piggle-Wiggle but the wicked, haughty Cruel Queen. On her head she wore a glittering jewelled crown. Her hair hung down her back in deep waves. Around her shoulders she had a purple fur-trimmed robe and on her face she wore a smile so cruel it made Kitty's teeth chatter. She stalked over to the bed and lay down. With her gold slippers she felt the bottom of the bed. With her ringed fingers she felt the top and the sides. She stood up and with her scepter she pulled back the spread to see if the pillows were wrinkled. Everything was perfect. The Cruel Queen's face became convulsed with fury. She yelled, "Not a wrinkle! Not a single lump! I am furious! But, never fear, little slaves, my day will come and into the dungeon you will go! Come, my servants, we will go." Mrs. Piggle-Wiggle stalked into the closet.

That was the beginning of Mrs. Piggle-Wiggle's friendship with the children. The next day Mary Lou and Kitty and Kitty's little brother, Bobby, and Bobby's friend, Dicky, went to Mrs. Piggle-Wiggle's for tea, and the next day they came and each brought someone else and pretty soon

every single child in town had been or was going to Mrs. Piggle-Wiggle's house.

She showed Bobby how to sneak out and get the fireplace logs without being caught by the Indians. She showed Dicky how a lawnmower is really a magic machine that mows down the enemy millions and billions at a time. She taught Max how to take out the ashes without making a sound and without leaving a trace to show the train robbers who were on his trail that he and the sheriff had camped there that night.

Mrs. Piggle-Wiggle certainly knew how to make work fun and she also knew that there are certain kinds of work that children love to do even though they do not know how very well. Like painting and ironing and cooking and carpentry.

One day at Mrs. Piggle-Wiggle's there were two little girls baking cookies; one little boy baking a pie and getting flour on the floor and eating most of the dough; a little girl ironing, in a very wrinkly fashion, all of Mrs. Piggle-Wiggle's clean clothes; four boys, with paint on their faces and feathers in their hair, chopping kindling; two boys painting the dog house; three little girls darning old pirate socks of Mr. Piggle-Wiggle's; and pirates, pirates everywhere, digging in the back yard, shooting and yelling, running through the house and grabbing hunks of raw cooky dough.

Mrs. Piggle-Wiggle was sitting over in a corner of the

living room sewing on doll clothes. She was wearing the jewelled crown and Kitty Wheeling was standing beside her throne, which was a chair with a table cloth draped over it, dipping her hairbrush in a glass of water and making Mrs. Piggle-Wiggle's hair into long wet curls.

Kitty said, "Your Highness, shall I use the gold or the silver hairpins?" Mrs. Piggle-Wiggle said, "Oh, let's use the ones with the diamonds in them, hairdresser, they look better with this crown." Just then the telephone rang and it was some mother wanting to know what to do with her little girl who wouldn't take a bath, and that is how Mrs. Piggle-Wiggle got started with her wonderful cures. She told Hubert's mother about the Won't-Pick-Up-Toys Cure; Patsy's mother about the Radish Cure; Allen's mother about the Slow-Eater-Tiny-Bite-Taker Cure; Anne and Joan's mother about the Fighter-Quarrelers Cure; Dick's mother about the Selfish-Boy Cure; Mary's mother about the Answer-Backer Cure; and Bobby and Larry and Susan's mother about the Never-Want-To-Go-To-Bedders Cure.

2

THE WON'T-PICK-UP-TOYS CURE

Hubert was a very lucky little boy whose grandfather always sent him wonderful toys for Christmas. Hubert's mother said that his grandfather sent him these marvelous presents because Hubert was such a dear little boy. His father said that it was to make up for that awful name they had wished on him. Hubert was named for his grandfather. His full name was Hubert Egbert Prentiss.

Hubert liked the presents his grandfather sent him, but who wouldn't? He had an electric train with track that went four times around his bedroom and into the closet and out again and had seven stations and every signal there was and two bridges and a snow shed. He also had a Little-Builder set so large that he could build regular office buildings; and a great big wagon full of stone blocks made into shapes so that he could build big stone bridges for his electric train and stone buildings and even stone barracks for his one thousand and five hundred toy soldiers. Hubert also had a circus with every kind of wooden, jointed animal and clowns and tightrope walkers and trapeze artists. He had a little typewriter, and a real desk and a little radio and two automobiles. He had about a hundred or more airplanes and little cars. He had a fire engine with real sirens and lights and hook and ladders; and so many books that he had to have two bookcases in his room.

Hubert liked all of his toys and he was moderately generous about letting other children play with them, but he never put his things away. When his mother made his bed she had to pick her way around and in and out and over the electric train and track. She had to take circus performers off the bureau and the bed posts. She had to pick up books that had been thrown face down on the floor and she was continually gathering up the Little-Builder set. It used to take her about three hours to do Hubert's room and about one hour to do the rest of her housework.

She would send Hubert up to put his toys away, but all he ever did was to stuff them under the bed or into the closet and in the morning when his mother cleaned his room, there they were for her to pick up.

Mrs. Prentiss was getting a little bored with this.

One rainy Saturday Hubert invited all of his little friends to play up in his room. He had Dicky and Charlie and Billy and Tommy and Bobby. They got out every single toy that Hubert owned and played with them and then, just before dinner, they all went home and left the mess. Hubert's mother didn't know a thing about this until the next morning when she went in to make Hubert's bed. Then she just stood in the doorway and looked. The electric train track went under the bed five times and under the bureau and under the chairs and around the desk and into the closet. All along the track were bridges and buildings of the stone blocks and whole towns built from the Little-Builder set. On the bed and under the bed and on the bureau were the circus tent, the animals, the clowns, the tightrope walkers and the trapeze artists. The floor was littered with books and little automobiles and airplanes and painting sets and chemical sets and woodburning sets and crayons and coloring books and the little typewriter and the printing set and teddy bears and balls and jacks and parchesi games and jigsaw puzzles and soldiers, soldiers, soldiers.

Perspiration broke out on Hubert's mother's forehead and she began to feel faint so she closed the door and slowly went downstairs.

She took two aspirin tablets and then telephoned her

friend, Mrs. Bags. She said, "Hello, Mrs. Bags, this is Hubert's mother and I am so disappointed in Hubert. He has such lovely toys—his grandfather sends them to him every Christmas, you know—but he does not take care of them at all. He just leaves them all over his room for me to pick up every morning."

Mrs. Bags said, "Well, I'm sorry, Mrs. Prentiss, but I can't help you because you see, I think it is too late."

"Why, it's only nine-thirty," said Hubert's mother.

"Oh, I mean late in life," said Mrs. Bags. "You see, we started Ermintrude picking up her toys when she was six months old. 'A place for everything and everything in its place,' we have always told Ermintrude. Now, she is so neat that she becomes hysterical if she sees a crumb on the floor."

"Well, I certainly hope she never sees Hubert's room," said Mrs. Prentiss dryly. "She'd probably have a fit." And she hung up the phone.

Then she called Mrs. Moohead. "Good morning, Mrs. Moohead," she said. "Does Gregory pick up his toys?"

"Well, no, he doesn't," said Mrs. Moohead. "But you know Gregory is rather delicate and I feel that just playing with his toys tires him so much that I personally see that all of his little friends put the toys away before they go home."

"That is a splendid idea," said Hubert's mother, "but I am trying to train Hubert, not his playmates."

"Well, of course, Hubert is very strong and healthy, but Gregory is intelligent," said Mrs. Moohead.

"Is he?" said Mrs. Prentiss crossly, because she resented this inference that her son was all brawn and no brain.

"Oh, dear," squealed Mrs. Moohead, "I think Gregory is running a temperature. I must go to him." She hung up the phone.

Mrs. Prentiss then called Mrs. Grapple. "Hello, Marge," she said. "How's Susan?"

Mrs. Grapple said, "I've spanked her seven times since breakfast and I just heard a crash so she is probably getting ready for another. How's Hubert?"

"That's what I called about," said Mrs. Prentiss. "Can you suggest a way to make Hubert *want* to pick up his toys? His room looks like a toy store after an earthquake."

"Why don't you call this Mrs. Piggle-Wiggle? I have heard she is perfectly wonderful. All the children in town adore her and she has a cure for everything. As soon as I spank Susan, I'm going to call her."

Hubert's mother said, "Thank you very much, Marge. That is just what I'll do. I had forgotten about Mrs. Piggle-Wiggle, but I just know she can help me."

So she called Mrs. Piggle-Wiggle and said, "Mrs. Piggle-Wiggle, I hate to bother you, but you seem always to know what to do about children and I'll confess that I don't know what to do to make Hubert put his toys away."

Mrs. Piggle-Wiggle said, "Hubert is the sweet little boy with all the wonderful toys that his grandfather sends him, isn't he?"

Mrs. Prentiss said, "Why, yes, but I didn't know that you knew him."

"Oh, yes," said Mrs. Piggle-Wiggle. "Hubert and I are old friends. In fact, he is building an automobile in my back yard out of orange crates and empty tomato cans. Hubert is a very good carpenter."

Hubert's mother thought of the two little automobiles with rubber tires, real horns, leather seats big enough for two boys and lights that turned on with a switch, that Hubert's grandfather had given him; and she wondered why in the world he would want to build an automobile out of old orange crates and tomato cans. She said, however, "So that is where he and Dicky go every afternoon. I certainly hope he behaves himself."

"Oh, he does," said Mrs. Piggle-Wiggle. "We are all very fond of Hubert. But this problem of his toys. Let me see." Mrs. Piggle-Wiggle was quiet for some time. Then she said, "I think that the best thing for you to use is my old-fashioned Won't-Pick-Up-Toys cure. Starting now, don't pick up any of Hubert's toys. Don't make his bed. In fact, do not go into his room. When his room becomes so messy he can't get out of it, call me." Mrs. Piggle-Wiggle said goodbye and hung up the phone.

Hubert's mother, looking very relieved, went gaily about her housework, baked a chocolate cake for dinner and did not say a word to Hubert when he came home with ten little boys and they all trailed upstairs to play in Hubert's room.

The next morning when Hubert came downstairs for breakfast his mother noticed that he had a little pan of water-color paint stuck in his hair and his shirt had purple ink from the printing set on one shoulder. She said nothing but tripped upstairs after breakfast and quickly shut the door of his room.

The next morning Hubert's mother had a little trouble shutting the door of his room and she noticed that Hubert had circles under his eyes as though he had not slept very well.

The next morning Hubert was very late coming downstairs and before he opened his door his mother heard a great clatter and scraping as though he were moving furniture. He had Little-Builder bolts stuck to his sweater and two paint pans in his hair. He was so sleepy he could barely keep his eyes open and he had a red mark on one cheek. His mother looked at it closely and saw that it was the shape and size of one of his stone blocks. He must have slept with his head on one of the bridges.

On the seventh day after Hubert's mother stopped putting away his toys, he did not come down to breakfast at all. About eleven o'clock his mother became worried and called up Mrs. Piggle-Wiggle.

She said, "Good-morning, Mrs. Piggle-Wiggle. This is the seventh day of the old fashioned Won't-Pick-Up-Toys cure and I am worried. Hubert has not come downstairs at all this morning."

Mrs. Piggle-Wiggle said, "Let me see! The seventh day —it usually takes ten days—but Hubert has so many toys he would naturally be quicker."

"Quicker at what?" asked Hubert's mother anxiously.

"Quicker at getting trapped in his room," said Mrs. Piggle-Wiggle. "You see, the reason Hubert hasn't come downstairs is that he cannot get out of his room. Have you noticed anything different about him lately?"

"Well," said Hubert's mother, "he looks as though he hadn't been sleeping well and on the fourth morning he had a red blotch on his cheek just the shape of one of his stone blocks."

"Hmmmmm," said Mrs. Piggle-Wiggle. "He probably can't get at his bed and is sleeping with his head on his blocks for a pillow."

"But what will I do?" asked Hubert's mother. "How will I feed him?"

"Wait until he calls for food, then tell him to open the window and you put a piece of rather dry bread and peanut butter on the garden rake. He will have to drink out of the hose. Tie it to the rake and poke it up to him."

When Hubert's mother hung up the telephone she heard a muffled shouting from the direction of Hubert's room. She hurried upstairs and listened outside the door. Hubert was shouting, "Mother, I'm hungry!"

His mother said, "Go over and open the window, dear. I will send something up to you on the rake."

Mrs. Prentiss took the crusty piece of a very old loaf of bread, spread some peanut butter on it and took it around to the side of the house. Pretty soon Hubert's window was raised about a foot and a hand and arm appeared. His mother stuck the bread on one of the tines of the rake and poked it up at the window. The hand groped around for a while and then found the bread and jerked it off. The window banged shut.

That night when Hubert's father came home his mother told him all about Mrs. Piggle-Wiggle's treatment. Hubert's father said, "Mrs. Piggle-Wiggle sounds all right, but none of this would have happened if Hubert's grandfather hadn't given him so many toys. When I was a boy all I needed to have a good time was a little piece of string and a stick. Why, I—"

Mrs. Prentiss said, "Not that old string-and-stick routine again, John. Anyway now that Hubert has the toys the picture is changed."

Mr. Prentiss hid his face behind the evening paper and said, "Something smells delicious. Is it Irish stew, I hope?"

"Yes, dear," said Hubert's mother worrying about how she was going to serve Irish stew to Hubert on a rake. She finally put a potato on one prong, a carrot on another, an onion on another and pieces of meat on the last three. The window was opened only about three inches but the hand grabbed the food. After dinner Hubert's father tied the hose to the rake and held it up while Hubert put his mouth to the window opening and tried to get a drink of water. It was not very successful but he managed to get a few drops.

Mrs. Prentiss was worried. The next morning she knocked on Hubert's door and said, "Hubert, what are you doing in there?"

Hubert said, "I've got a bear pen made out of bureau drawers and my bed's the mother bear's house and my train runs under my bed thirteen times now."

"Hubert, dear, don't you think you should try and come out soon?" asked his mother.

Hubert said, "I don't wanna come out. I like it in here. All my toys are out and I can play with them any old time I wanna. This is fun."

His mother went downstairs and called Mrs. Piggle-Wiggle. Mrs. Piggle-Wiggle said, "Oh, but he will want to come out. Wait and see."

That afternoon about two o'clock there was music on the street and children's voices laughing and calling and pretty soon, right past Hubert's house, marched Mrs. Piggle-Wiggle and all the children and right behind them came the circus parade. Hubert managed, by putting one foot in a bureau drawer and the other in a freight car of his train, to get up to the window and look out. He waved to Mrs. Piggle-Wiggle and she called, "Hurry, hurry, Hubert! We are going to march all over town and then we are all going to the circus."

Hubert turned around quickly with the idea of getting

to the door and joining the fun, but the freight car went scooting under the bed and the bureau drawer tipped over and hit him smartly on the shins. Hubert began to cry and to try and kick his way to the door. But everything he kicked seemed to hit back. He kicked a building and a big block fell on his toe. He kicked at a Little-Builder office building and it fell over and clouted him on the back of the head. He kicked a book and it hit a lamp which fell and knocked a heavy wooden elephant off the bedpost onto Hubert's shoulder. He could hear the music of the circus parade growing fainter and fainter and so he bawled louder and louder.

Then he heard a tapping at his window. He crawled over and reached out. It was the rake with a note on it. He took the note and opened it. It said:

> The only way you can get out of that trap
> is to put everything away where it belongs.
> If you hurry we will wait for you.
>> Your friend,
>>> Mrs. Piggle-Wiggle

Hubert began by finding the Little-Builder box. He took down an office building and put each piece in its right place. Then he put away the stone blocks, then the train tracks, the circus, the soldiers, the paints, the chemical set, the printing press, the books, the fire engines, the automobiles. He played little games, pretending that he was racing someone to see who could find the most parts of a game the quickest.

He had to take off the bedclothes and shake them in order to find the soldiers and the circus and then he thought that as long as the bedclothes were off anyway, he might as well make his bed. It was so lumpy when he finished he thought he had left some airplanes in it and took the covers off again and shook them. He made the bed again and this time it was neat and smooth. Hubert was proud.

He was under the desk finding the last piece of the Little-Builder when he heard the music again. He put the piece in the box, put the box in the closet and tore down the stairs and out the front door.

There they came, Mrs. Piggle-Wiggle, all the children and the CIRCUS! Hubert ran out to meet them and nobody said anything about the pan of orange paint stuck in his hair or the word XYPGUN printed on his cheek in purple ink.

Away they went down the street, Hubert carrying the flag and yelling the loudest.

3

THE ANSWER-BACKER CURE

At three o'clock in the after-
noon Mrs. O'Toole put a peanut butter sandwich and a nice
cool glass of milk on the kitchen table for her little girl
when she came home from school. Pretty soon the front door
slammed and in bounced Mary, her red braids switching
like little pony tails. Her mother said, "How was school,
darling?"

Mary said as she gulped her milk and took a large bite of
the sandwich, "Well, this afternoon, Miss Crabtree said,
'Mary O'Toole will stay in at recess and put the paint boxes
away,' and I said"—Mary took another gulp of the milk—

37

" 'You're the teacher here, Miss Crabtree, why don't you put away the paint boxes and let me go out and play?' Everybody in the whole room laughed but mean old Miss Crabtree, and she sent me into the cloak room."

Mary took another large bite and looked up at her mother expectantly to see if she would appreciate how smart she was.

However, her mother said, "That was a very rude thing for you to do, Mary, and I am ashamed of you. When you finish your sandwich and milk you had better go up to your room and stay until dinner. You can concentrate on how rude you were to nice Miss Crabtree."

Mary pulled her mouth down at the corners, squinted up her pretty brown eyes and said, "Why should I?" She kept her mouth pulled down and blinked her eyes rapidly in a most disagreeable way.

Mrs. O'Toole was dumbfounded. Never had her little Mary acted in this horrid way before. She said quietly, "You should because I tell you to, now scat."

Mary walked slowly out of the kitchen switching her skirt and her braids and managing to look impudent even from the back. When she reached the top of the stairs, she called down to her mother, "I'm going because I want to but not because you tell me to," and dashed into her room and banged the door.

That night at dinner, Mary was quite normal but after dinner her daddy said, "Scoot the dishes off the table,

WeeUn. Your mammy's tired," and his dear little WeeUn instead of jumping up and doing what she was told, pulled her mouth down until she looked like a sad Jack-o-Lantern, squinted up her eyes and said, "I'll do it because I want to but not because you tell me to. Anyway, you eat here, why don't you clear the table?" She blinked her eyes rapidly.

Her father looked as though he might be going to give her a spanking, but then he noticed that it was time for the news so instead he went into his study, turned on the radio and lit his pipe.

Mary did clear off the table and she dried the dishes but she kept blinking her eyes and muttering.

The next morning her mother said, "Please hurry with your breakfast, Mary. The children are waiting and you'll make them late for school."

Mary pulled her mouth down and began blinking. She said, "I'm the one that's eating this breakfast, madam!" (She pronounced it "mattam".) Mary's mother sighed and said, "If you only knew how unattractive you look when you talk like that, you would stop right now."

Mary mumbled something into her mush, then grabbed her sweater and slammed out the front door.

Mrs. O'Toole went to the telephone and called her friend Mrs. Ragbag. She said, "Hello, Mrs. Ragbag, have you noticed any change in Calliope lately?"

Mrs. Ragbag said, "Well, no, I can't say I have, Mrs. O'Toole. She seems to be studying hard in school and she eats and sleeps well. Have you noticed anything wrong with her?"

Mrs. O'Toole said, "No, it is not Calliope I'm worried about. It is Mary. Yesterday afternoon she came home from school and she seemed perfectly normal and she looked all right, but she told me how very impudent she had been in school. I punished her, of course. In fact, I sent her to her room to stay until dinner but she was impudent to me. She was rude to her father, too. I just cannot understand it. I thought perhaps all the children were acting this way. She pulls down her mouth, squints up her eyes and blinks. She looks hideous."

Mrs. Ragbag said, "Oh, I am sorry, Mrs. O'Toole, because Mary has always been such a dear little girl. I don't know what to suggest. Why don't you call Mrs. Keystop, you know what a problem her little Chuckie is. She should have some ideas."

Mrs. O'Toole said, "Thank you very much, Mrs. Ragbag, I'll call Mrs. Keystop right now."

So she called Mrs. Keystop but she wasn't at home and the maid, Norah, answered the phone. Norah said, "Sure and Mrs. Keystop ain't home, Mrs. O'Toole, but how is that dearrrrrr little Marrrrrry, the one with the beautiful brrraids?"

Mrs. O'Toole said, "Oh, Norah, that is just why I called. Mary has suddenly become so impudent. She answers back and she pulls her mouth down and squints up her eyes and blinks. She started yesterday and I'm so upset. I called to ask Mrs. Keystop if she has ever had similar trouble with Chuckie."

Norah said, "Sure and there ain't any trrrouble she hasn't had with that Chuckie. He's so rude he talks back to himself, but I'm thinkin' you'd best call Mrs. Piggle-Wiggle. That little woman has forgotten morrre about children than we'll everrrr know. She even taught Hubert Prentiss to pick up his toys. Now therrrrre's a spoilt child."

Mrs. O'Toole said, "Oh, thank you so much, Norah. I should have thought of Mrs. Piggle-Wiggle in the first place. I'll call her right now."

Mrs. O'Toole called Mrs. Piggle-Wiggle and said, "Oh, Mrs. Piggle-Wiggle, I am so worried about my little girl, Mary."

Mrs. Piggle-Wiggle said, "I know Mary. She has such beautiful red hair and such lovely brown eyes."

Mrs. O'Toole said, "Well, she still has the hair anyway, but her eyes don't look pretty any more. She squints them up, pulls down her mouth and then blinks."

Mrs. Piggle-Wiggle said, "She answers back and is impudent, isn't she?"

Mrs. O'Toole said, "Yes, she is. But how did you know? I do hope that she hasn't been rude to you."

Mrs. Piggle-Wiggle said, "Oh, no, Mary is always very polite to me, but I can recognize the Answer-Backer symptoms. When was she first impudent?"

"Yesterday afternoon right after school. She was rude to dear Miss Crabtree, her teacher, and when I sent her to her room she made this hideous face and said, 'I'll do it because I want to but not because you tell me to!' Mrs. Piggle-Wiggle, she walks in such a way that her braids twitch and even her back looks impudent."

Mrs. Piggle-Wiggle said, "Don't worry so, Mrs. O'Toole. Some of the most charming children I know were once Answer-Backers. Fortunately Mary has only just begun so she can be cured in no time at all. You drop by here after lunch and I will give you Penelope Parrot to keep for a while. Mrs. Garrison has been using Penelope but she has had her for a month now and Garry should be cured by this time. Now, don't worry, Mrs. O'Toole. Penelope is a cure for even the most stubborn cases of Answer-Backish-ness."

Mrs. O'Toole hung up the phone and she felt much better. Right after lunch she went down to Mrs. Piggle-Wiggle's house and got Penelope. Penelope Parrot was a large, cross-looking green bird who blinked rapidly. Mrs. Piggle-Wiggle said, as she handed the cage to Mrs. O'Toole, "Fortunately for you, Penelope will only talk to children."

During the walk home from Mrs. Piggle-Wiggle's house Penelope was quiet in a very cross, blinky-eyed sort of way and when Mrs. O'Toole hung her cage in the kitchen, she hunched down and put her head under her wing. But when

Mary came in from school, Penelope woke up and began preening her feathers. Mary was delighted with Penelope. She said, "Oh, Mother, I've always and always wanted a parrot. Do you think she can talk?"

Mrs. O'Toole said, "She hasn't said a word since I brought her home but I was told that she speaks only to children."

Mary said, "Where did you get her, Mother? Is she for me? May I have her in my room for my very own?"

Her mother said, "I am keeping her for a friend of mine but when you play in your room, you may hang her cage by the window."

Mary brought her milk and cookies over by Penelope's cage and was very surprised when Penelope blinked and said rudely, "Gimme a bite, pig!" Mary broke off a piece of the cookie and poked it through the bars of the cage. Penelope snatched it and said, "Thanks, pig!"

Mary turned to her mother. "She's certainly not very polite, is she?"

Her mother said, "Perhaps she has been around rude people. After all she is only a parrot and repeats what she hears."

Penelope blinked her eyes and said, "Oh, yeah? Oh yeah? Oh yeah?" Mrs. O'Toole looked a little shocked but Mary laughed and said, "May I bring the children in to see her, Mother. May I?"

Before Mrs. O'Toole could answer, Penelope began hopping up and down, blinking and yelling, "Say are you the boss around here? Are you the boss around here? Are you the boss around here?"

Mary's mother said, "I am the boss around here, Penelope, and if you are not more courteous, I'll put a cloth over your cage."

Penelope blinked and muttered.

Mary bounced up and down excitedly. "What will that do, Mother? What will that do to Penelope?"

Mrs. O'Toole said, "If I put a cloth over her cage, she will think that it is night and go to sleep."

Penelope squawked, "I'll do it because I want to but not because you tell me to!"

Mary was certainly surprised at that because she thought that she had made up that brilliant remark. She didn't dare to look at her mother so she put on her sweater and went out to find her playmates.

Pretty soon she came back with five little friends and they spent the afternoon standing around Penelope's cage and laughing at her rude remarks.

This worried Mrs. O'Toole. If Mary thought Penelope was so amusing then perhaps she would imitate her and become ruder than ever. So she called Mrs. Piggle-Wiggle. She said in a low voice so the children in the kitchen could not hear, "Mrs. Piggle-Wiggle, I am rather worried because although Penelope is very rude to the children, they don't mind at all. Mary thinks she is very funny and laughs at everything she says."

Mrs. Piggle-Wiggle said, "Just remember, Mrs. O'Toole, that this is only the first day with Penelope. Let Mary be with her as much as she wishes. Keep Penelope's cage in the breakfast nook when Mary eats her lunch and breakfast and in the dining room at night. Hang her cage in Mary's bedroom when she goes up there to play and have Penelope sleep in Mary's room. I am sure that you do not have to worry. Penelope has never failed me."

Mrs. O'Toole said, "All right, Mrs. Piggle-Wiggle. I'll do just as you say. Goodbye!"

Just before dinner Mrs. O'Toole said to Mary, "Mary, dear, send your little friends home now. It is time for you to set the table." Mary turned to her mother and began pulling down her mouth, squinting her eyes and blinking but before she could say a word, Penelope yelled out, "Say who's the boss around here? Who's the boss around here? Who's the boss, anyway?"

Mary's mother quickly put a cloth over her cage, politely asked the children to leave and sent Mary in to set the table.

When Mr. O'Toole came home from the office, she took the cover off again to show him the parrot and then she hung Penelope in the dining-room window. After dinner Mary's daddy said, "Up on your toes, Miss Molly O'Toole, and scoot the dishes out to the kitchen."

Mary pulled down her mouth, squinted up her eyes,

blinked her eyes but Penelope said, "What am I, a servant? Work! Work! Work! What am I, a servant? Say who's the boss around here?"

Mary's daddy laughed so hard the tears ran down his cheeks, but Mary stuck out her tongue at Penelope who bounced around yelling, "Only snakes stick out their tongues! Only snakes stick out their tongues!"

Mary pulled her tongue in quickly and shut her lips together tight. My, but she thought Penelope was horrid!

Mrs. O'Toole hung Penelope's cage in Mary's room and Penelope squawked and made so much noise that Mary finally said, "Oh, be quiet!" And Penelope blinked and said, "I'll do it because I want to but not because you tell me to. I'll do it because I want to but not because you tell me to."

Mary flounced into bed and turned off the light.

The next morning Mary was very slow. She could not find one of her socks and she couldn't button her dress and finally her mother called, "Mary, hurry, dear, breakfast is waiting!"

Mary pulled down her mouth and squinted up her eyes and said, "Oh, hurry, hurry, hurry. Hurry yourself!"

Penelope had been preening her tailfeathers but when she heard Mary she jerked her head up and said, "Oh, hurry, hurry, hurry. Hurry yourself, slowpoke. Hurry yourself, slowpoke. Hurry slowpoke! Hurry slowpoke! Hurry slowpoke! Hurry, hurry, hurry, hurry!"

Mary said crossly, "Oh, be quiet, Penelope!"

Penelope said, "I'll do it because I want to but not because you tell me to. Say, who's the boss around here? Oh, yeah? Oh yeah? Oh yeah?"

Mary ran downstairs and sat down to breakfast leaving Penelope still shouting, but Mrs. O'Toole ran upstairs and got Penelope and hung her cage by the kitchen window.

When the children called for Mary and Mrs. O'Toole said, "Hurry, dear, you will make your friends late for school," Mary pulled down her mouth and squinted up her eyes and blinked but before she could say a word, Penelope squawked, "I'm the one who's eating this breakfast, mattam! Hurry, hurry, hurry, that's all I hear. Hurry yourself, slow-poke!"

Mary was ashamed to look at her mother, so she rushed off without kissing her goodbye. Penelope yelled after her, "Hurry slowpoke. Bell's ringing! Bell's ringing!"

When Mary came home from school that afternoon she kissed her mother and said, "Mother, I apologized to Miss Crabtree, today, and she said that next week I may be monitor for the scissors."

Penelope yelled, "Who said so? Who said so? Who said so? Who's the boss? Who's the boss?"

Mary turned to Penelope and said, "You are a very rude bird. If you don't hush right now I will put the cloth over your cage."

Penelope blinked and said, "Hush, hush, hush! That's all I hear. I'll do it because I want to but not because you tell

49

me to. I'll do it because I want to but not because you tell me to. Who's the boss around here, anyway?"

Mary's mother said, "I am the boss and I think it is time you went home, Penelope. Mary would you like to return Penelope to Mrs. Piggle-Wiggle?"

Mary said, "Oh, yes, Mother. And may I stay and play?"

Mrs. O'Toole said, "I think you had better come home and practise. Your music lesson is tomorrow, you know."

Mary started to draw down her mouth, squint up her eyes and blink but suddenly she looked at Penelope and so she turned up her mouth, opened her eyes and smiled. She said, "All right, Mother. I'll come right home *after* I return that rude Penelope."

4

THE SELFISHNESS CURE

Dick Thompson was certainly a nice-looking boy and he was smart in school and behaved well at the table BUT whenever his name was mentioned, people said, "Poor, poor, Mrs. Thompson. She has such a problem. Whatever will she do with that child?"

I guess that you would feel simply dreadful if people said a thing like that when your name was mentioned, but Dick didn't. You see, Dick Thompson was a selfish, greedy boy and he cared more about being a selfish, greedy boy than about what people said.

When children came over to his house to play, Dick said,

"Don't touch that, that's MINE! You can't play with that, that's MINE! Put down MY ball. Take off MY skates!"

Each time this happened—at least each time it happened where his mother could hear Dick saying, "That's MINE!" —she would send him up to his room to think about how selfish he was. Dick would go right upstairs for he was very obedient, but instead of thinking how bad it was to be selfish he would sit on the bed and swing his legs and think, "Everything in this room is MINE and nobody is going to touch MY things!"

He certainly was a problem.

One day Dick's mother bought a big box of peppermint sticks. She called Dick into the house and said, "Now, dear, I have bought this large box of peppermint sticks for you, but I want you to share them with your friends. There are about fifty sticks in the box and I want you to divide them with all the children in the neighborhood. Don't forget the *little* children, Dick, and you might send one or two to Old Mrs. Burry, she is so fond of peppermint."

Dick said, "Thank you, Mother, for the fine candy." Then he took the box out of doors and put it in the basket on the front of his bicycle and allowed the neighborhood children to look at the peppermint sticks, but he warned them, "This is MY candy and if anyone touches it I will hit him with MY baseball bat!"

The children in his neighborhood had known Dick for some time and they knew that he meant what he said, but as they looked at the candy they wished and wished they could have just one stick. Dick's mother, watching from the window, saw all the children gathered around Dick and the box of candy in the basket on the front of his bicycle and she thought to herself, "Just look at my little Dick. Dividing the candy with all of his little friends. I just knew he would learn to be generous," and she tapped on the window and when Dick looked around she waved and smiled at him.

Dick waved and smiled back, but unfortunately just then Mary O'Toole, who was quite daring, reached in and grabbed a stick of the candy and CRACK! Dick clouted her on the hand with the baseball bat. In a flash his mother saw what was really going on. She flew out the front door, took Dick firmly by the arm and marched him upstairs, thrust him into his room and slammed the door. Then she went downstairs and out the front door, took the box of candy and told Mary O'Toole to divide it up among all the children, even the little ones and to take one or two sticks over to old Mrs. Burry because she was so fond of peppermint.

There were fifteen children, not counting Dick, and fifty sticks of candy so each child was given three sticks and old Mrs. Burry got five.

From the window of his bedroom, Dick watched Mary divide the candy and he was just furious.

After all the candy had been divided, Mrs. Thompson went into the house and called Dick's father. She said,

"Herbert, I know that you are busy and you don't like to have me call you at the office, but I'm so worried about Dick."

Dick's father said, "What is the matter? Is he sick?"

Dick's mother said, "No, but I just wish he were. It would be so much simpler."

Mr. Thompson said, "Now, dear, I am very busy so perhaps you had better wait until I come home."

Mrs. Thompson said, "Herbert, this cannot wait another minute," and she told him about the candy and the baseball bat.

Mr. Thompson said, "Why not give him a good hard spanking? Tell him that you are going to give him something that he can keep all to himself. Ha, ha!"

"Now, Herbert, this is not a laughing matter and I don't think a spanking will solve a thing. I just don't know what to do or which way to turn," and Mrs. Thompson began to cry, partly because she felt so humiliated over Dick's selfishness and partly because she knew that crying was one way to get action out of Dick's father.

Dick's father said, "Now, now, dear, tears won't help. Let me see—shall I hop into a taxi and come home and thrash Dick?"

Dick's mother only cried louder.

Dick's father said, "I know. I know just what to do. Call that Mrs. Wriggle-Spiggle or whatever her name is. You know, the one who cured Hubert Prentiss."

"You mean Mrs. Piggle-Wiggle. Oh, Herbert, you are so wonderful! I knew you would think of something. I'll call her right away," and Mrs. Thompson blew her nose and cheered right up.

Mothers always do cheer up when they think of Mrs. Piggle-Wiggle because she knows so much about children. After all, she has had about a thousand little boys and girls come to her house to pull taffy, play checkers, bake cookies, drink cambric tea and dig for the pirate gold buried in her back yard, and so she has had plenty of opportunity to learn about childish ailments and the cures for them. She was certainly the person to ask about Dick, the selfish boy, and so Mrs. Thompson telephoned her. She said, "Hello, Mrs. Piggle-Wiggle, this is Mrs. Thompson, Dick's mother."

Mrs. Piggle-Wiggle said, "Hello, Mrs. Thompson, I have rather expected you to call."

Mrs. Thompson said, "You have? Why?"

"Because I know Dick very well," said Mrs. Piggle-Wiggle, "and although he is a dear little boy and the most well-mannered child who comes to visit me, never once forgetting to say Thank you and Please, he is very selfish."

"Oh, I know he is. I know he is," said Mrs. Thompson almost crying because she was so ashamed that Mrs. Piggle-Wiggle should know how selfish Dick was.

Mrs. Piggle-Wiggle said, "Now, Mrs. Thompson, do not feel sad. Selfishness and greediness are just diseases like measles and chickenpox and can be cured very easily but we must start now, before another day passes, because Dick is such a nice little boy and we want everyone to like him as we do."

"Oh, do you like him, in spite of his selfishness?" asked Dick's mother.

"Of course, I do," said Mrs. Piggle-Wiggle. "I love all children but it distresses me when I see a child who has a disease like Selfishness or Answerbackism or Won't-Put-Away-Toys-itis and his parents don't do a thing to cure him."

"But I want to cure Dick," said his mother. "I will do anything to cure him."

Mrs. Piggle-Wiggle said, "The Selfishness Cure is really very simple, but the rules must be followed very strictly. You will have to come down here and get my Selfishness Kit and at the same time I will give you the directions for its use."

"Thank you so much, dear Mrs. Piggle-Wiggle," said Mrs. Thompson. "I will leave right now," and she hung up the phone, slipped on a jacket and ran all of the way to Mrs. Piggle-Wiggle's house.

When she arrived Mrs. Piggle-Wiggle was on the front porch waiting for her. On the porch beside her was quite a large green metal box with SELFISHNESS KIT painted on its side in white letters. Mrs. Piggle-Wiggle invited Dick's mother to sit down and then she opened the kit.

Inside were about twenty-five padlocks of various sizes. There were great big ones about the size of apples, down to little tiny ones not much larger than a penny. Also there were screws and a screw driver; a box of cloth labels that said DICK; a box of blank gummed labels; a small can of white paint; a small can of black paint; a small paint brush; and a pastry bag—this is a large bag with a nozzle on the end which, when filled with frosting, can be squeezed and the frosting comes out the end like toothpaste and can be formed into words.

Mrs. Piggle-Wiggle said, "Mrs. Thompson, these padlocks are for Dick's drawers, his closets, his toy chest, his bicycle, his bedroom door, his night-stand drawer and his toothbrush. As soon as you get home put the padlocks on everything he owns and give him the keys. This is to assure him that HE and HE ALONE can touch HIS things. The name labels are to be sewn in all of his clothes and the gummed stickers are to be put in all of his books—even his school books—notebooks, pencil boxes, and are to be pasted on his ruler, crayons and paints. On each sticker print in large letters with this black paint DICK'S BOOK—DON'T TOUCH! DICK'S NOTEBOOK—DON'T TOUCH! and so forth.

"On every toy he owns you must paint in either black or white paint, DICK'S BALL—DON'T TOUCH! or DICK'S BAT—DON'T TOUCH. Put the name of the toy first and then Don't Touch.

57

"The pastry bag is to be filled with a simple white frosting and used to mark Dick's sandwiches, his fruit, his cookies and his plate for each meal.

"That's all there is to it. I expect you will be returning the Selfishness Kit before a week has passed."

Mrs. Thompson said, "I do hope so, Mrs. Piggle-Wiggle. Are you sure it will work?"

"It has cured hundreds of other children and I see no reason why it should not cure Dick. A week or even less, I should say."

Mrs. Thompson thanked Mrs. Piggle-Wiggle very much and then, lugging the kit, she walked home. As soon as she had hung up her jacket she began sewing the labels in all of Dick's clothes. He asked her what she was doing and when she showed him he was as happy as could be. "Boy, that will just show people who owns MY clothes," he said proudly.

Mrs. Thompson did not answer but continued to put the labels on every single stitch of his clothing including his socks and his handkerchiefs. Then she opened the kit and took out the tiniest padlock. She fastened Dick's toothbrush to the toothbrush rack with the little padlock, snapped it shut and handed the key, which was not much bigger than a pin, to Dick. "You had better find a ring to hold your keys," she said. "You are going to have about twenty-five of them."

"Boy, that's just wonderful!" Dick said fondling the tiny

key and thinking, "That's MY toothbrush, and now nobody but ME can touch it." He was very happy.

When dinnertime came Mrs. Thompson closed the Selfishness Kit and took it downstairs to show Dick's father. She told him about Mrs. Piggle-Wiggle and he patted her on the back and said that he was sure everything was going to be all right and where was the evening paper.

After dinner they went upstairs to put some of the padlocks on and were surprised to find that Dick, himself, had already put the locks on each of his bureau drawers, his night-stand drawer, his toy box, his closet door and his bedroom door. He had also put stickers on the covers of all of his books, notebooks, coloring books, crayon and colored-pencil boxes, and stamp album. On the stickers he had printed in black paint DICK'S BOOK—DON'T TOUCH! DICK'S NOTEBOOK—DON'T TOUCH! DICK'S CRAYONS—DON'T TOUCH! DICK'S PENCIL BOX—DON'T TOUCH! DICK'S STAMP ALBUM—DON'T TOUCH! He was very proud and asked his father if he didn't think he printed well.

His father said, "You should be able to print well, you have certainly practised enough," and he looked disgustedly around the room at the stickers which labeled everything— DICK'S BRUSH—DON'T TOUCH! DICK'S COMB —DON'T TOUCH! DICK'S WINDOW BLIND— DON'T TOUCH!

He turned to Dick's mother and said, "Perhaps we should

wear stickers, DICK'S MOTHER—DON'T TOUCH!
DICK'S FATHER—DON'T TOUCH! I'll bet he'll wear
monogrammed underwear when he grows up."

Mrs. Thompson said, "Oh, I hope not, Herbert."

Dick said, "Come on, Mom and Dad, let's mark all the
rest of my stuff."

And so they worked until 8:30, marking Dick's bicycle,
his baseball, his bat, his pitcher's glove, his catcher's glove,
his tool box, his roller skates, his lunchbox, his rubber boots,
his raincoat, his Indian suit, his soldier suit, his gun, and his
wagon. They even painted DICK'S DOG—DON'T
TOUCH! on Rover's collar.

When they had finished and it was time for Dick to go
to bed, he kissed his mother and said goodnight to his father
and went happily up the stairs, his ring of keys jingling
from his belt.

Mr. Thompson sank down into a chair in the living room
and lit his pipe. "I trust that Mrs. Piggle-Wiggle knows
what she is doing," he said, "because if this cure should not
work, our son, Dick, is going to be the most loathsome boy
in the whole world."

Mrs. Thompson said, "Oh, no, dear, not in the whole
world!"

The next morning they heard Dick clicking and snap-
ping at his padlocks long before they were up. He was a
little late coming downstairs because it took time to padlock all of his drawers, his closet door and the door of his

room, but he was very happy and his mother noticed that he had pinned one of the name labels on the outside of his sweater. While he was eating his breakfast marked DICK'S BREAKFAST—DON'T TOUCH, his mother marked his sandwiches DICK'S SANDWICHES— DON'T TOUCH, and his apple DICK'S APPLE— DON'T TOUCH! and his cookies DICK'S COOKIES— DON'T TOUCH! His lunchbox had already been marked DICK'S LUNCHBOX—DON'T TOUCH!

After breakfast Dick put the lunchbox in the basket on his bicycle and noticed proudly the large sign hanging from the crossbar, DICK'S BICYCLE—DON'T TOUCH!

At school the children paid little attention to the sign on his bicycle but when he opened his lunchbox and took out the sandwiches marked DICK'S SANDWICHES— DON'T TOUCH! and the apple marked DICK'S APPLE —DON'T TOUCH and the cookies marked DICK'S COOKIES—DON'T TOUCH! everyone laughed and wanted to see them and in the resulting crowding and push- ing one of the sandwiches was dropped and stepped on and some of the big boys grabbed the apple and tossed it in the air just above Dick's head shouting, "Throw me DICK'S APPLE. Oh, look, I dropped DICK'S APPLE! I wonder if DICK'S APPLE will bounce." When they finally gave Dick his apple it was bruised and very dirty.

In arithmetic period that afternoon, Bobby Slater across the aisle asked Dick for his ruler and when he saw the label

DICK'S RULER—DON'T TOUCH! he began to laugh and reached over and snatched the ruler off Dick's desk and passed it to Kenny Hatch who laughed and passed it to the girl in front of him and finally Miss Crabtree had to come down and get it. When she saw the sign she laughed, too, but she gave the ruler back to Dick.

After school the boys decided to play baseball in the vacant lot by Dick's house but when Dick brought out his bat and ball and mitts and the boys saw DICK'S BALL—DON'T TOUCH! DICK'S BAT—DON'T TOUCH! they said, "We can't touch anything so let's go home," and they did.

Dick went up to his room to play but he found that somewhere during the day he had lost the key to his closet and that he had locked the key to his toy chest in the chest so he went down and sat on the front porch and listened to the shouts of the children playing in Hubert Prentiss' yard.

The next morning at school during recess nobody would play with him and the little girls followed him and laughed. When they marched into school the children pointed and laughed and laughed and Miss Crabtree came down to see what the trouble was and she almost laughed herself when she saw the sign someone had pinned on the back of Dick's sweater. It said "THIS IS DICK—DON'T TOUCH!"

At lunch time the children crowded around to watch him take out his sandwiches and one little girl said, "He's so

selfish and greedy he has his sandwiches marked so he can't share them." Then the children danced around him and chanted, "Dick's sandwich—Don't touch! Dick's apple— Don't touch! Dick's lunchbox—Don't touch!" Finally Dick took his lunchbox out and put it in the basket on his bicycle but the children followed him and seeing the big sign DICK'S BICYCLE—DON'T TOUCH! they yelled and laughed and sang, "Dick's—don't touch! Don't touch Dick! Dick's—don't touch! Don't touch Dick!"

After school Dick hurried right home, but he had lost the key to his room so he went down to the basement to play with his tool box but every time he saw the large white sign DICK'S TOOLBOX—DON'T TOUCH! he thought of school and the lunchbox and he remembered how the children laughed and jeered and he was ashamed. At dinner when his mother brought him his plate marked DICK'S DINNER—DON'T TOUCH! he said, "Aw, why do you hafta mark my plate? I don't care which one I get."

Mrs. Thompson looked significantly at Mr. Thompson and said, "All right, Dick, we won't mark your plate if you will share your dessert with Rover."

Dick thought for a few minutes and then he carefully broke his chocolate cake into two equal pieces and gave one to Rover who gulped it down and looked grateful.

After dinner Dick told his father he had lost the keys to his room and the closet and so his father took off the padlocks on those doors and on the toybox. Dick said, "Don't put them back, Dad, I don't care who goes into my room or gets into my stuff."

The next morning Dick got up early and scraped the DICK'S LUNCHBOX—DON'T TOUCH! from his lunchbox and took the sign off his bicycle. Then he went in to his mother and said, "Mom, please don't mark my sandwiches. Please, don't mark any of my stuff, Mom." Mrs. Thompson said, "All right, Dick, I only did it to protect you."

Dick said, "I don't care who gets my lunch. Just don't mark it."

At noon all the children gathered around Dick but neither his sandwiches, nor his apple, nor his lunchbox were marked so they rushed out to see his bicycle but there was no sign on it, so they sat down and ate their lunches.

Right after school that night Dick hurried home and scraped the marking off his ball and bat and mitts and then he walked up to where the children were playing ball and tossing the ball, bat and mitts down beside the catcher he said, "Do you want to use these? I don't care," and he went back to his own house.

In a little while Mary O'Toole rang the doorbell and asked Mrs. Thompson if Dick could come out and play. Mrs. Thompson said, "He'd love to, Mary, but first he must return something to Mrs. Piggle-Wiggle."

Mary said, "Tell him to come over to the lot when he gets back and here are some keys he lost."

Mrs. Thompson said, "Thank you for the keys, dear, but thank goodness they belong to Mrs. Piggle-Wiggle, not to Dick."

She took the keys of the big padlocks and the tiny padlock up to Dick who was in his room, busily packing Mrs. Piggle-Wiggle's Selfishness Kit.

5

THE RADISH CURE

Up to the time of this story Patsy was just an everyday little girl. Sometimes she was good and sometimes she was naughty but usually she did what her mother told her without too much fuss. BUT ONE MORNING Patsy's mother filled the bathtub with nice warm water and called to Patsy to come and take her bath. Patsy came into the bathroom but when she saw the nice warm tub of water she began to scream and yell and kick and howl like a wild animal.

Naturally her mother was quite surprised to see her little girl acting so peculiarly but she didn't say anything, just took off Patsy's bathrobe and said, "Now, Patsy, stop all this nonsense and hop into the tub."

Patsy gave a piercing shriek and ran from the bathroom stark naked and yelling, "I won't take a bath! I won't ever take a bath! I hate baths! I HATE BATHS! I haaaaaaaaaa-aaaaate baaaaaaaaaaaths!"

Patsy's mother let the water out of the tub and went downstairs to telephone her friends and find out if their children had ever behaved in this unusual fashion; if it was catching and what to do about it.

First she called Mrs. Brown. She said, "Hello, Mrs. Brown. This is Patsy's mother and I am having such a time this morning. Patsy simply will not take a bath. Pardon me, just a minute, Mrs. Brown."

She put down the telephone receiver and went over to Patsy who was standing in the kitchen doorway listening to the telephone conversation and feeling very important.

Patsy said, "What did Mrs. Brown say to do with me, Mother?"

Patsy's mother said, "She hasn't told me yet but while I am finding out you had better march right upstairs and get dressed and then you can pick up that messy, sticky pasting work you left all over your room last night. Don't come downstairs until every single thing is put away."

Patsy's mother picked up the telephone and Mrs. Brown said, "I'm sorry but I can't offer any suggestions because our little Prunella just adores to bathe. Perhaps Mrs. Grotto could help you."

So Patsy's mother called Mrs. Grotto. She said, "Hello, Mrs. Grotto, I just called to ask if you could help me with Patsy. She won't take a bath and I am at my wits' end."

Mrs. Grotto said, "Well, frankly, I don't know what to suggest because our little Paraphernalia simply worships her bath. Of course, Paraphernalia is quite a remarkable child anyway. Why, Thursday afternoon she said. . . ."

"Yes, yes, I know," said Patsy's mother quickly. "Goodbye, Mrs. Grotto, thank you anyway."

Then Patsy's mother called Mrs. Broomrack. "Good morning, Mrs. Broomrack," she said a little too brightly. "I wonder if you would do me a favor?"

"Why, of course, dear, of course!" said Mrs. Broomrack.

"Well," said Patsy's mother, "this morning for the first time in her life, our little Patsy won't take a bath. The very idea seems to make her hysterical and I don't know what to do."

Mrs. Broomrack said, "Why, you poor dear, all alone in that big house with that unmanageable child. Personally, I don't know what to say because our little Cormorant looks forward so to taking a bath. Bathing is his favorite pastime. In fact, sometimes we can't get him out of the tub."

"Why don't you let him stay in, then?" said Patsy's mother.

"Because he might drown!" squealed Mrs. Broomrack.

70

"Well . . ." said Patsy's mother, as she hung up the phone.

By this time she was feeling rather depressed because it seemed that bathing was the most popular indoor sport with every child in town but her own dirty little girl.

In desperation she decided to call Mrs. Piggle-Wiggle. "She should know about children," thought Patsy's mother. "She certainly has her house crawling with them, day and night."

It certainly was fortunate for Patsy's mother that she thought of Mrs. Piggle-Wiggle, because although Mrs. Piggle-Wiggle has no children of her own and lives in an upside-down house, she understands children better than anybody in the whole world. She is always ready to stop whatever she is doing and have a tea party. She is glad to have children dig worms in her petunia bed. She has a large trunk full of scraps for doll clothes and another trunk full of valuable rocks with gold in them. She is delighted to have children pick up and look at all the little things which she keeps on her tables and when Hubert Prentiss dropped the glass ball that snowed on the children when you shook it, she said, "Heavens, Hubert, don't cry. I'm so glad this happened. For years and years I have wanted to know what was in that glass ball." Mrs. Piggle-Wiggle takes it for granted that you will want to try on her shoes and go wiggling around on high heels.

Which is probably why she was not at all surprised when

73

Patsy's mother told her about the bath. "I suppose we all come to it sooner or later," she said. "Well, from my experience I would say that the Radish Cure is probably the quickest and most lasting."

"The radish cure?" said Patsy's mother.

"Yes," said Mrs. Piggle-Wiggle. "The Radish Cure is just what Patsy needs. All you have to do is buy one package of radish seeds. The small red round ones are the best, and don't get that long white icicle type. Then, let Patsy strictly alone, as far as washing is concerned, for several weeks. When she has about half an inch of rich black dirt all over her and after she is asleep at night, scatter radish seeds on her arms and head. Press them in gently and then just wait. I don't think you will have to water them because we are in the rainy season now and she probably will go outdoors now and then. When the little radish plants have three leaves you may begin pulling the largest ones."

"Oh, yes, Patsy will probably look quite horrible before the Radish Cure is over, so if you find that she is scaring too many people or her father objects to having her around, let me know and I will be glad to take her over here. You see, all of my visitors are children and dirt doesn't frighten them."

Patsy's mother thanked Mrs. Piggle-Wiggle very, very much for her kind advice and then called up Patsy's father and told him to be sure and bring home a package of radish seeds. Early Red Globe, she thought they were called.

The next morning she didn't say one single word to Patsy about a bath and so Patsy was sweet and didn't act like a wild animal. The next day was the same and so was the next and the next.

When Sunday came Patsy was a rather dark blackish gray color so her mother suggested that she stay home from Sunday School.

Patsy's father, who by this time had been told of the Radish Cure, didn't say anything to Patsy about washing but he winced whenever he looked at her.

By the end of the third week they had to keep Patsy in doors all of the time because one morning she skipped out to get the mail and the postman, on seeing her straggly, uncombed, dust-caked hair and the rapidly forming layer of topsoil on her face, neck and arms, gave a terrified yell and fell down the front steps.

Patsy seemed quite happy though. Of course, it was getting hard to tell how she felt as her face was so caked with dirt that she couldn't smile and she talked "oike is—I am Atsy and I on't ake a ath." She also had to take little teeny bites of food because she couldn't open her mouth more than a crack.

Naturally her father and mother had to stop having any friends in to visit except in the evening when Patsy was in bed and even then they were not at all comfortable for fear Patsy would wake up and call, "Ing e a ink of ater, Addy!" (Really, "Bring me a drink of water, Daddy.")

At last, however, the day came when Patsy was ready to plant. That night when she was asleep her mother and father tiptoed into her room and very gently pressed radish seeds into her forehead, her arms and the backs of her hands. When they had finished and were standing by her bed gazing fondly at their handiwork, Patsy's father said, "Repulsive little thing, isn't she?"

Patsy's mother said, "Why, George, that's a terrible thing to say of your own child!"

"My little girl is buried so deep in that dirt that I can't even remember what she looks like," said Patsy's father and he stamped down the stairs.

The Radish Cure is certainly hard on the parents.

Quite a few days after that Patsy awoke one morning and there on the back of her hand, in fact on the backs of both hands and on her arms and on her FOREHEAD were GREEN LEAVES! Patsy tried to brush them off but they just bent over and sprang right up again.

She jumped out of bed and ran down the stairs to the dining room where her mother and father were eating breakfast. "Ook, ook, at y ands!" she squeaked.

Her father said, "Behold the bloom of youth," and her mother said, "George!" then jumped up briskly, went over to Patsy, took a firm hold of one of the plants on her forehead and gave it a quick jerk. Patsy squealed and her mother showed her the little red radish she had pulled. Patsy tried to pull one out of her arm, but her hands were so caked with dirt that they couldn't grasp the little leaves so her mother had to pull them.

When they had finished one hand and part of the left arm, Patsy suddenly said, "Other, I ant a ath!"

"What did you say?" asked her mother, busily pulling the radishes and putting them in neat little piles on the dining room table.

"I oo want a b . . b . . . ath!" said Patsy so plainly that it cracked the mud on her left cheek.

Patsy's mother said, "I think it had better be a shower," and without another word she went in and turned on the warm water.

Patsy was in the shower all that day—she used up two whole bars of soap and she didn't even come out for lunch but when her father came home for dinner, there she was, waiting for him at the door; clean, sweet and smiling, and in her hand she had a plate of little red radishes.

6

THE NEVER-WANT-TO-GO-TO-BEDDERS CURE

Each evening as the clock struck eight, Mrs. Gray called Bobby and Larry and Susan. She said, "Come, children, eight o'clock and time for bed." She tried to make her voice sound cheerful and gay but actually she felt like groaning, because she knew what was coming.

First Susan, "Oh, we don't want to go to bed now. Please let us stay up a little while longer. Pleeeeeeeeeeese, Mother. Pleeeeeeeeeeeeese!"

Then Bobby, "We are the ooooooooooonly ones in our whoooooooooole neighborhood who have to go to bed at eight o'clock!"

Then Larry, "Mother, nobody, not anybody at aaaaaaaa-aall goes to bed at eight o'clock."

Then Susan again, "But, Mother, we have ooooooooonly just staaaaaaaarted this game."

Then Bobby, "Pleeeeeeeeese let us finish this game. *Pleeeeeese!*"

Then Larry, "Just one more turn, Mother. It's my turn, Mother, and I haven't won a game this evening—pleeeeee·eeeeeese!"

Mrs. Gray said, "Now, Bobby, Larry and Susan, you know that if you want to grow up into fine young men and women you must have plenty of sleep. I'm sure they teach you that in school."

"We don't wanna grow up, we just wanna finish this game," Bobby wailed.

And so night after night poor Mrs. Gray argued and pled, and begged her children to go to bed and by the time they had finished whining and complaining it was usually almost nine o'clock. Mrs. Gray was desperate.

Finally one day she called her friend, Mrs. Grassfeather. She said, "Hello, Mrs. Grassfeather, this is Mrs. Gray, and I would like to find out what time Catherine and Wilfred go to bed."

Mrs. Grassfeather said, "Why at eight o'clock, Mrs. Gray, unless their Uncle Jasper comes for dinner and then I usually let them stay up until nine-thirty to hear Uncle Jasper tell about his experiences in the Boer War. That, of course, is strictly Mr. Grassfeather's idea. He not only allows the children to stay up until nine-thirty but he pays them as well for listening to Uncle Jasper while he goes to bed."

Mrs. Gray said, "Do the children like to go to bed at eight o'clock?"

Mrs. Grassfeather said, "Oh, they are very good about it because they know that if they whine and complain I will not let them stay up the next time Uncle Jasper comes over, which is about four nights a week."

As the Grays had no Uncle Jasper, Mrs. Gray realized that Mrs. Grassfeather could be of no help, so she said goodbye and hung up the phone.

Then she called Mrs. Gardenfield. "Hello, Mrs. Gardenfield, this is Mrs. Gray and I called to see what time Worthington and Guinevere go to bed at night."

Mrs. Gardenfield said, "Oh, they go to bed any time after Daddy comes home. You see, Mrs. Gray, Mr. Gardenfield gets home at four-thirty, we have dinner at five-thirty, and the children, Mr. Gardenfield and I all go to bed at six-thirty."

"Six-thirty!" said Mrs. Gray, amazed. "My goodness, that *is* early!"

Mrs. Gardenfield said, "It is not early if you get up at four-thirty."

Mrs. Gray said, "But who wants to get up at four-thirty?"

"We do," said Mrs. Gardenfield and hung up the phone in a huff.

So Mrs. Gray thought and thought and suddenly she remembered that only yesterday Dick Thompson's mother had been telling her about a wonderful little woman named Mrs. Piggle-Wiggle and so, even though she had never seen Mrs. Piggle-Wiggle, she decided to call her on the telephone and ask her to help with her Never-Want-To-Go-To-Bedders.

She said to Mrs. Piggle-Wiggle, "I am Mrs. Gray, the mother of Bobby, Larry and Susan."

Mrs. Piggle-Wiggle said, "Oh, yes, of course. How are the children? I have not seen them since they returned from camp."

Mrs. Gray said, "Mrs. Piggle-Wiggle, Bobby and Larry and Susan are very well and very cooperative until about eight o'clock at night and then they turn into whiny, complaining little non-cooperators."

Mrs. Piggle-Wiggle said, "Oh, yes, I see. They are Never-Want-To-Go-To-Bedders, aren't they?"

Mrs. Gray said, "How on earth did you know?"

Mrs. Piggle-Wiggle laughed and said "Oh that is one of the commonest of the children's ailments. The moment you said they were good until eight o'clock I knew what the trouble was."

Mrs. Gray said, "Do you know anything to do for them? How to cure this hateful disease?"

Mrs. Piggle-Wiggle said "Oh that's very simple. Beginning tonight, don't tell them to go to bed. Let them stay up as late as they want to. You and Mr. Gray go on to bed any time you are tired but leave the children downstairs."

Mrs. Gray said "But their health? That will ruin their health!"

Mrs. Piggle-Wiggle said "Oh I do not believe that a day or so without sleep will harm them and it will certainly cure them. It is really worth a try, Mrs. Gray, but if you have any trouble and the cure doesn't seem to be working, call me."

Mrs. Gray said, "Oh, thank you so much, Mrs. Piggle-Wiggle. I will let you know tomorrow how we are getting along."

That night at eight o'clock the clock struck and Mrs. Gray continued to mend socks and said nothing about bed and Mr. Gray changed the radio and Bobby and Larry and Susan played parchesi.

At nine o'clock the clock struck again and Mrs. Gray put down the socks and took up a woman's magazine. Mr. Gray changed the radio and Bobby and Larry and Susan continued to play parchesi.

When ten o'clock struck, Mrs. Gray yawned and put down the magazine, Mr. Gray snapped off the radio and Larry and Susan and Bobby began another game of parchesi.

At ten-thirty Mr. and Mrs. Gray went upstairs to bed and left the children playing parchesi.

At twelve o'clock Mrs. Gray awoke and at first thought

there were burglars in the house, then she remembered the Never-Want-To-Go-To-Bedders so she tiptoed down the stairs and there were Bobby and Larry and Susan playing parchesi on the living-room rug.

The next morning the children slept until eleven-thirty. About nine o'clock Dick Thompson's mother stopped by to take them to the beach but Mrs. Gray told her they were still asleep.

When the children finally got up they were cross and quarrelsome. When their mother told them about Mrs. Thompson inviting them to the beach they said, "Why didn't she wait for us? Why didn't you wake us up? I think Mrs. Thompson's mean not to wait."

Mrs. Gray said, "I see no reason why Mrs. Thompson and Dick should have their day spoiled waiting for the three little members of the All-Night Parchesi Club to get up. Now come and eat your breakfast and stop complaining."

That night after dinner Mr. and Mrs. Gray went to a moving picture show and left Larry and Bobby and Susan playing tiddly-winks. When the Grays came home about twelve-thirty the children were still up playing tiddly-winks and quarreling about whose turn it was.

The next morning they had a nine o'clock dentist appointment and so Mrs. Gray got them up at eight. Susan was so sleepy she could not eat her mush and Larry yawned so much he choked on his egg and had to be turned upside down and shaken by his legs. Bobby just sat and rubbed his eyes.

Bobby went to sleep in the car on the way to the dentist, Susan went to sleep in the dentist's waiting room and Larry slept all the way home.

That night, after their parents had gone to bed, Larry said, "Why do we hafta stay in the house for all the time? Let's go outside and play."

So they went outside and put on their roller skates and began skating up and down on the dark streets.

Mrs. Milgrim who lived on the corner came out on her front porch in her bathrobe and yelled, "For heaven's sake, don't you children know that it is almost midnight? What on earth are you doing up at this hour?"

Larry said, "We don't have to go to bed any more. We stay up late every night."

Mrs. Milgrim said, "Well, stay up some place else. And be QUIET!" She went into the house and slammed the door.

So the children took off their skates and tiptoed back to the house. They got out the parchesi board but Susan said it was her turn for the pinks and Larry said, "I happen to beg your pardon, but it is my turn."

Susan said, "You had the pinks yesterday and Bobby had them the day before and it's my turn tonight," and she began to cry.

Larry threw the pinks at her and one of them went into the fireplace and they had to strain the ashes through their fingers until they found it. When they finally were ready to play, Bobby was asleep with his head on the board, so Susan and Larry played, jumping their men across Bobby's head, until Susan too fell asleep right in the middle of her turn. Larry woke Susan and Bobby and they all went to bed just as the clock struck one.

The next day there was a matinee at the neighborhood theatre and Mrs. Gray said they could go. It was a wonderful picture, with Indians and cowboys and pioneers, and the children were very excited. But, no sooner had they found their seats and settled back in the nice dark theatre when first Susan, then Bobby and finally Larry fell asleep. They slept peacefully through the Indian picture, a Mickey Mouse cartoon and a newsreel. When the show was over all the other children went home to dinner but Larry and Susan and Bobby slept on. Susan was the first to awake. She sat up and rubbed her eyes. Where was she? Why was it so dark? Oh, how stiff and cramped she was. She poked Larry and Bobby until they too awoke. They were frightened when they realized that they were still in the theatre, now dark and empty, except for two rats nibbling popcorn in the front row. Susan began to cry, "Everybody's gone and left us and we'll have to stay in here until we die," she bawled. Larry said, "Oh, Susan, don't be so silly. All we have to do is walk out the door. Come on, everybody." They groped their way up the aisle to the door but it was locked. They tried all the doors but they were all locked.

Susan began to cry again. "I'm hungry and I want to go home," she wailed.

Bobby said, "I'll bet there's a back way, Larry. Let's look."

They felt their way back down the aisle again and climbed up on the stage. Then suddenly they heard the front door open, a flashlight's bold eye blinked in the darkness and a voice said, "Hey, what's goin' on here? What are you kids doing?"

It was Mr. Murphy, the janitor, and the children were so glad to see him that they ran and clung to his legs and all talked at once. "Oh, Mr. Murphy, we were locked in. We must have fallen asleep in the picture. What time is it? Will you let us out?"

Mr. Murphy laughed at them, let them out the front door and drove them home. Mother and Daddy were in the living room playing bridge with the Andersons and seemed not at all surprised to see the children. Mrs. Gray said, "There's bread and milk on the kitchen table. Please put everything away, when you finish," and went on with her game.

The children ambled out to the kitchen but they were too tired to eat so they went upstairs and flung themselves across their beds. After they had rested for a while Larry suggested that they play burglar. They turned off all the upstairs lights and crept around behind doors and under beds and had a fine scary time until Larry pushed Bobby down the clothes chute and Bobby stuck and Susan screamed and Daddy came upstairs and yanked Bobby out, spanked them all and sent them to their rooms. Susan and Bobby got right into bed and went to sleep but Larry stayed awake until the guests had gone home and their mother and daddy had gone to bed, then he pinched Bobby awake and they both sneaked into Susan's room and pulled off her covers. Larry said, "Let's go downstairs and see if there are any sandwiches or cookies left." Susan was very sleepy but she said, "Oooooooh, aaaaaall right."

They ate about ten little sandwiches, a small dish of salted nuts, two little dishes of candy, some olives and pickles and some chocolate marshmallow cake. They felt very lively after that so they sat down at the bridge table and began playing slapjack. When they finished the last game the birds were singing and they heard the thump of the morning paper on the porch. They scurried up to bed quickly.

The next day was Patsy's birthday. It was a wonderful party with a fishpond and a magician who did tricks and games and balloons and prizes for every child. But Larry and Bobby and Susan did not enjoy it at all. Susan had such big black circles under her eyes that Patsy's mother thought she was sick and would not let her have any refreshments. Bobby was so sleepy he fell asleep just as the magician pulled a rabbit from under his chair and the magician thought Bobby was so rude he gave the rabbit to Hubert Prentiss. Larry fell asleep right at the table. He laid his cheek in his ice cream, closed his eyes and dreamed he was in the North Pole. Patsy's mother called all the others to look at him and he awoke very embarrassed.

Mrs. Piggle-Wiggle

That night, when eight o'clock came, Mr. and Mrs. Gray were working on the budget and not saying much and Susan and Larry and Bobby were sitting on the davenport pinching each other to keep awake. At last the clock struck— bong, bong, bong, bong, bong, bong, bong, bong! The children jumped up and rushed over to their mother and father. They said, "It is eight o'clock and time for bed. Please let us go to bed. Please don't make us stay up any more. Pleeeeeeeese!"

Mrs. Gray said, "Why I thought you enjoyed staying up late. I thought all the children in this neighborhood stayed up late."

The children said, "Nobody has to stay up late but us. We just hate it. May we go to bed, pleeeeeeeese?"

Mrs. Gray said, "Very well, children, from now on, if you are good, I will let you go to bed at eight o'clock every night."

7

THE SLOW-EATER-TINY-BITE-TAKER CURE

Once upon a time there was a little boy named Allen. He had curly brown hair and sturdy legs and a very shiny smile. One morning he sat down to breakfast, but instead of picking up his spoon and eating his mush and milk like a good little boy he took a fork and began eating his cereal grain by grain.

When his mother, certain that he had eaten all of his mush, brought him his egg, he was still on the eleventh grain of cereal.

Allen's mother said, "My goodness, you are poky this morning, dear. What is the matter? Is the mush too hot?"

Then she noticed that Allen was eating his cereal with a fork so she took the fork away and handed him the spoon saying, "Now, then, eat properly and hurry or your egg will get cold."

Allen took the spoon but instead of filling it with mush he daintily lifted one grain from the bowl and slowly brought it up to his mouth. His mother watched him for a few minutes and then said, "Well, eat an ice cold egg, if you like, *but* I am going upstairs to sort the laundry and when I come down I want to find every bit of that mush and all of the egg eaten."

Allen's mother went skipping upstairs and left Allen in the breakfast nook. As soon as his mother left the kitchen Allen picked up the fork again and began eating his mush by the grain. In a little while even a whole grain seemed too much so he broke each grain in two, taking only half grains on the fork tines. He was so interested in his little bitty bites that he didn't hear his mother come in and was very surprised when she suddenly whisked away his breakfast and sent him marching up to his room.

At lunchtime Allen's mother made cream of tomato soup. This was Allen's very favorite soup but Allen, instead of eating it up quickly and asking for more, began floating little specks of cracker in the bowl. He floated, chased and ate them one by one.

At two o'clock his mother stopped the little cracker

crumb chase, sadly cleared the table and sent Allen up for a nap.

At dinner that night, Allen cut his meat into such small pieces that his father looked over at him and said, "Perhaps you would like to borrow my magnifying glass? I am sure you are going to need it to see those infinitesimal bits of meat."

Allen's mother said, "He has been like that all day. Eating his mush grain by grain with a fork; floating tiny cracker crumbs in his soup and chasing and eating them one by one and now this meat. What is the matter with you, Allen?"

Allen smiled his shining smile and said, "I guess I'm just a slow eater. I choke if I take larger bites."

His mother said, "Nonsense! You were all right yesterday."

Allen said sadly, "Yes, Mother, but that was yesterday," and he carefully cut a grain of corn into four pieces and delicately put the smallest piece into his mouth.

The next morning he had not improved a bit and though his mother scolded and scolded, he took the smallest slowest bites imaginable and to make matters worse he sighed and gazed around the room between each bite.

Allen's mother was very distressed and not knowing what else to do, she called her friend, Mrs. Crankminor.

"Good morning, Mrs. Crankminor," said Allen's mother. "This is Allen's mother and I called to ask if you have ever had any difficulty with Wetherill about eating?"

"Difficulty?" said Mrs. Crankminor. "Just what kind of eating difficulty?"

"Well," said Allen's mother, "Allen has suddenly taken to eating so slowly that if I didn't take his plate away, I'm sure that it would take him approximately twelve hours to eat an average meal. He eats his cereal grain by grain, his soup drop by drop and his meat pore by pore."

"Goodness, gracious, is the child ill?" asked Mrs. Crankminor.

"No, he says that he feels well and I have taken his temperature and it is normal. I don't know what the trouble is," said Allen's poor worried mother.

Mrs. Crankminor said, "I certainly have no complaint about Wetherill's eating. My only difficulty is in getting him to stop. Yesterday morning before breakfast, he weighed one hundred and eighty-two pounds and his father has begun calling him Blimpy."

"Oh, my," said Allen's mother, "I guess you have a more serious problem than I have," and she hung up the phone.

Then she called her friend Mrs. Wingsproggle. "Mrs. Wingsproggle," she said, "do you have any trouble with Pergola at mealtimes?"

Mrs. Wingsproggle said, enunciating very carefully, "Noooo, not eggsactly, trouble, but we do have to keeup after her to chew each mouthful one hundred tie-ums. Some-tie-ums she is forgetful and only chews her food about ninety-thrrrrrrrrreee tie-ums and one day I caught her stopping at seventy-one."

Allen's mother could already picture how disastrous it might be if Allen heard that Pergola Wingsproggle chewed each bite one hundred times because if she multiplied each grain of mush in a dish by one hundred and took into account the unbelievable slowness with which Allen was able to chew, she realized that he would die of slow starvation before a day had passed. Allen's mother hurriedly said goodbye to Mrs. Wingsproggle and hung up the phone.

Then she called Patsy's mother. She said, "Does Patsy eat everything that is put before her quickly and without urging?"

Patsy's mother said, "Yes, she does, why?"

Allen's mother said, "Because Allen has taken to eating like a scared mosquito, and I don't know what to do."

Patsy's mother said, "Call Mrs. Piggle-Wiggle. She'll know what to do. You remember the Radish Cure, don't you?"

Allen's mother was delighted. She said, "Oh, of course, I do and I'll call Mrs. Piggle-Wiggle right now," and she did.

Mrs. Piggle-Wiggle said, "So Allen has become a Slow-Eater-Tiny-Bite-Taker, has he? I thought he looked a little pale this afternoon."

Allen's mother said, "He is so pale his father calls him his little doughboy, and I know that he hasn't eaten more than a tablespoon of food in the last two days. What will I do, Mrs. Piggle-Wiggle?"

Mrs. Piggle-Wiggle said, "Don't worry about Allen, he'll be all right again in a day or two. Let me see, is it, yes, it is Allen coming down the street right now, so I'll send home the Slow-Eater-Tiny-Bite-Taker dishes with him.

"Use the largest set for Allen's dinner tonight; the medium size for his meals tomorrow; the small size the next day and the very small dishes the last day. Serve him portions of food to fit the dishes. That will be four days in all, counting today, and though he may lose some weight, he will gain it right back. I may send for him on the last day and no matter how he feels, let him come to my house."

Allen's mother said, "Thank you, very much, Mrs. Piggle-Wiggle. I will do just as you say and I will be so happy when he is cured."

"I will send Allen right home with the dishes," said Mrs. Piggle-Wiggle. "Now don't worry. Simply follow my instructions," and Mrs. Piggle-Wiggle said goodbye.

After a little while Allen came home carrying a large wicker basket. "Here's a present from Mrs. Piggle-Wiggle, Mother, and she said for me to be very careful with it." He set the basket on the kitchen floor and commenced to undo the fastenings. His mother said, "No, dear, this is a present for me and I think I'll just put it aside for now. You run out and play until dinner. Goodness, you are pale. Run as fast as you can down to Patsy's house and put some roses into your cheeks."

Allen's mother put the basket on the top shelf in the kitchen and shut the cupboard door which left nothing for Allen to do but go out and play. However, instead of running down to Patsy's, he walked very, very slowly because he was tired from not having had enough to eat.

Just before dinner, Allen's mother took down the basket and opened it. There were four little sets of dishes. The largest set had a plate the size of a saucer, a cup like a small after-dinner coffee cup, a small fork and a little spoon.

The medium size set had a plate like a doll plate, a doll cup, a very small fork and spoon.

The small size set had a plate the size of a silver dollar, a cup like a thimble, a fork like a match and a spoon like a salt spoon.

The tiny size set had a plate the size of a penny, a cup that would hold but a drop, a fork like a needle and a spoon like a pin.

Allen's dinner that night was served on the large set. He was given a baked potato as small as an egg, a piece of meat like a postage stamp, a slice of tomato, and the small cup of milk. Allen was so interested in taking tiny bites that he didn't even notice his new dishes. He ate one third of the potato, one sixth of the meat, one tomato seed and drank about half a cup of milk.

When he asked to be excused, his father looked at his saucer plate still heaped with food and started to say "NO!" but Allen's mother quickly said, "Yes, dear, you may be excused but you must play in your room until bedtime."

The next morning his mother put a teaspoon of scrambled egg and an inch-square piece of toast on the medium size plate and a tablespoon of orange juice in the doll cup. Allen loved the tiny fork and spoon because he was able to take such small bites that in one hour he had eaten but half the egg and one third of the toast. He did drink all of the orange juice.

At luncheon and dinner he ate even less and took even smaller bites. He had turned a very pale green and was so tired he had to sit down all of the time.

The next day his mother brought out the small dishes. On the dollar plate she put three cornflakes, a piece of bacon the size of a snowflake, and a quarter of a teaspoon of egg. In the thimble cup she put ten drops of cocoa.

Allen was so tired that he had to crawl in to breakfast on his hands. He was happy about the tiny dishes, though, and gave his mother a very sickly edition of the shiny smile. He cut the cornflakes into thirteen pieces and ate a part of one. He ate a speck of egg, a nibble of bacon and five drops of cocoa and then crawled in and lay on the couch.

For lunch he had seven drops of soup, two cracker crumbs and enough milk to barely moisten his lips.

For dinner he ate one lima bean and drank four drops of

milk. He crawled up to bed right after dinner. He had to rest eight times on the way upstairs.

The next morning he was so tired it took him almost half an hour to crawl down to breakfast. His mother had the penny plate, the drop cup and the needle fork and pin spoon. On the penny plate she had one grain of egg, two toast crumbs, and two raspberry jam seeds. She had a drop of milk in the cup. Allen was so weak he had to lift the needle fork with both hands but even so he cut the one grain of egg in two and ate only one of the toast crumbs. He drank half the drop of milk and then lay down on the breakfast nook bench.

Just then the telephone rang and it was Mrs. Piggle-Wiggle for Allen. His mother had to carry him to the telephone and hold the big heavy telephone receiver. Mrs. Piggle-Wiggle had great difficulty in hearing his weak squeaky voice and finally had to give up and talk to his mother. Mrs. Piggle-Wiggle said, "It is Allen's turn to exercise the spotted pony and I would like him to come over here right away."

Allen's mother told Allen and he was very excited but he was so weak that his mother had to carry him out and put him in his little red wagon. Fortunately it was downhill all the way to Mrs. Piggle-Wiggle's house and when he got there Dick Thompson and Hubert Prentiss were waiting for him out in front. They lifted him out of his little red wagon and laid him across Spotty's back. Spotty turned his head around and licked the top of Allen's head comfortingly. Mrs. Piggle-Wiggle came out onto her front porch to see him off and it took much self-control for her to keep from laughing as Spotty started slowly off down the street with Allen lying on his back like a bag of cornmeal. All morning Allen lay on Spotty's back, his face buried in his mane, while Spotty paced the streets. Several times women rushed out of their houses and asked Allen if he was ill, if he needed any help. Allen was very embarrassed and squeaked out, "I'm all right," and tried to sit up but he was too weak.

When twelve o'clock came Allen was so tired that he knew he could not stay on Spotty's back another minute so he guided the pony up to his own front gate. Then he rolled off his back onto the grass. He lay there like a wet sock, bawling.

His mother looked out the kitchen window and seeing him lying there she became frightened. She thought Spotty was a spirited horse and that he had bucked Allen off. She ran out and knelt beside him. "Darling," she said, "are you hurt? Did that vicious horse throw you? How many times did he buck?"

Allen smiled weakly at the idea of gentle little Spotty bucking or throwing anyone, but then he began to cry again as he remembered that this was his last chance for a long time to exercise Spotty and he was so weak that he couldn't stay on his back. He finally said to his mother, "Spotty did not buck or throw me. It is just that I am so tired I cannot stay on his back. I rolled off and now I can't get back on and it's my turn to exercise him and I won't have another turn for a long, long tiiiiiiiiiiIIIME!"

Allen's mother said, "Now, see here, Allen. This all comes from your turning into a Slow-Eater-Tiny-Bite-Taker and if you want to ride Spotty this afternoon, you will have to come into the house and eat something."

She tied Spotty to the fence, picked Allen up, carried him into the house and set him in the breakfast nook. He leaned weakly back against the wall and closed his eyes.

His mother began rattling pans and turning on burners and pretty soon she handed him the drop cup filled with cream of tomato soup and the penny plate with two cracker crumbs on it.

She said, "Now drink this soup in one gulp and put BOTH those crumbs in your mouth at once." Allen did as he was told then leaned back and closed his eyes again.

Then his mother handed him the thimble cup filled with milk and a tiny peanut butter sandwich on the dollar plate. She said, "Drink this milk in one swallow and put that whole sandwich in your mouth." Allen did and was surprised to find that he didn't feel quite so tired. He leaned back but he kept his eyes open.

Then his mother handed him the doll cup filled with soup and the doll plate with some cottage cheese on it. "Drink that soup right down," she said, "and here is a large

fork and I want that cottage cheese eaten in two bites."
Allen did as he was told. My, but he was feeling strong! He
could sit up without leaning back and oddly enough he was
very hungry.

His mother handed him the after-dinner coffee cup filled
with milk and the saucer plate with a piece of gingerbread
on it. Allen didn't have to be told how to eat and drink these.
He took large hungry bites and big swishing gulps and the
dishes were empty. His mother said, "Do you feel better,
dear? Have you had enough lunch?"

Allen said, "I feel much better, Mother, but I'm still very
hungry. May I please have a large bowl of soup and a large
glass of milk?"

"Of course, dear," said his mother and she quickly filled
a large bowl with soup and a large glass with milk. Allen
ate every drop of soup and drank every drop of milk and
then jumped up from the table saying, "Oh, Mother, I bet
Spotty's hungry. Shall I take him some soup?"

"No, dear," said his mother. "I think that Spotty would
prefer an apple and some lumps of sugar." So they fed
Spotty and then Allen climbed on his back and rode
proudly away, sitting up very straight and holding on to
the reins with one hand.

When he reached the corner by Patsy's house his mother
called him to come back. He turned Spotty around and
steered him up to the gate and his mother came out with
the basket of Slow-Eater-Tiny-Bite-Taker dishes. "Would

you mind returning these to Mrs. Piggle-Wiggle?" she asked.

"Not at all," said Allen graciously. "Just hand me the basket. I'll put it here in front of me and hold it with this hand. You see, Mother, I only use one hand to steer now."

He carefully arranged the basket, kissed his mother, clucked to Spotty, and away they went, in a very slow walk, toward Mrs. Piggle-Wiggle's house.

8

THE FIGHTER-QUARRELERS CURE

Joan Russell opened her blue eyes and saw that it was morning. She saw also that her twin sister, Anne, was still asleep. Joan reached over and gave Anne a little pinch. "Wake up, Anne!" she said making her voice scary and urgent. "Wake up quickly, there's a big black spider in the bed and it's on your side."

Anne awoke with a squeal, leapt out of bed, stubbed her toe on the box of paints she had left on the floor the night before, banged her funny bone on the door and went screaming into her mother's and father's room. "Mother, Daddy, there's a big black spider in our bed on my side! Motherrrr-rrrrrr! Daaaaaaaaaady!"

Mrs. Russell sighed, sat up and reached for her robe. She said in a low, calm voice, "Anne, you didn't fall for that old trick again, did you?"

Anne grabbed her mother's arm and jumped up and down, squealing, "But Mother, Joan said so. It's a big black spider!"

Mr. Russell turned over and yawned. He said, "Ohhhhh, aaah! Stop jumping and squealing and listen. *If* there is a big black spider in the bed, and it is highly unlikely, then, WHY is Joan lying in there, staring at the ceiling and waiting to be bitten AND TO BE SPANKED!" he added in a loud voice.

Anne stopped squealing and listened gravely to her father but when he finished speaking she said, "But Joan said there was a spider, Daddy. She said there was!"

Her daddy said, "Last one dressed gets the littlest melon!" and he jumped out of bed and chased Anne out of the room, roaring like a lion.

Mr. Russell sang gaily in his shower but Mrs. Russell frowned as she dressed, for from the children's room she could hear, "That's my sock! Give it to me!"

" 'Tis not. It's mine! Give it back!" (*sound of slap*)

"Mother, Anne's slapping me!"

"That's my petticoat. You're putting on MY petticoat. Give it to me!"

" 'Tis not. It's mine!" (*sound of slap*)

"That's mine!"

"No, that's mine!"

" 'Tis not."

" 'Tis too!"

Slap, bang, crash, running steps. "MOTHERRRRRRR!"

Mrs. Russell said to herself, "Quarreling, quarreling, from the minute they get up until they go to bed at night. I do not believe that I can stand another day of it." She ran downstairs and began jamming the oranges into the squeezer.

Mr. Russell came whistling in to breakfast. He said mildly, "Oh, scrambled eggs again. I was hoping for sausages and buckwheat cakes."

Mrs. Russell said, "We had sausages and buckwheat cakes yesterday morning."

Mr. Russell said, "What about brook trout? Bill Smith has 'em nearly every morning."

Mrs. Russell said crossly, "Perhaps that is why he looks like a trout and his wife looks like a great big halibut."

Mr. Russell peered at her over the top of his morning paper. He said, "You know, sweetheart, I think that the children's fighting and quarreling is making you irritable."

Mrs. Russell said, "I think it is too. In fact, it is driving me crazy. Just listen to them."

From the upper hall they could hear, "It's my turn to go down first, Joan!"

" 'Tis not, it's my turn!"

"You were first yesterday, you know you were."

"But last night you traded your first turn for my pink crayon."

"I did not!"

"You did too!"

"Cheater!"

"Double cheater!"

In came the twins. Joan looked at her melon and then at Anne's. She said, "Anne's melon is the biggest. She always gets the biggest and the most of everything."

Anne said, "You had the biggest yesterday. You're just a pig. You always want the most."

Their daddy said, "As a matter of fact, ladies, I have the biggest melon because I was the first one dressed. NOW HUSH!" He glared at them.

The twins sat meekly down to their breakfast. They had taken but two bites, however, when Anne poked Joan and hissed, "I've got the most cereal. Ha, ha, ha!"

Joan hissed back, "Yes, but I have three pieces of bacon and you have only two."

Anne looked and sure enough Joan did have three pieces. She grabbed one but Joan snatched her wrist and in the ensuing scuffle they managed to tip over Anne's milk and spill it all over the front of their nice blue pleated skirts. Their daddy spanked them. Their mother sponged them off and they left for school, red-eyed and miserable, but still quarreling. As they rounded the corner their mother could hear, "That big tablet is mine!" " 'Tis not." " 'Tis too!"

After Mr. Russell had left for the office, Mrs. Russell picked up the telephone and called her friend Mrs. Quitrick. She said, "Mrs. Quitrick, this is Mrs. Russell, the twins' mother, and I want to know if Jasper and Myrtle ever quarrel."

"Oh, my dear," said Mrs. Quitrick, "all children quarrel. Why yesterday Myrtle hit Jasper with her big doll and the eyes came out and then Jasper hit Myrtle with the little hammer out of his nice new tool box and the head came off the hammer and I just told them that I wouldn't have them breaking up their toys that way."

Mrs. Russell said, "But the children, weren't they hurt?"

Mrs. Quitrick said, "Why, I didn't notice. I was so angry at them for breaking their lovely toys and the doll hospital won't be able to put Myrtle's doll's eyes back for two weeks and you know how hard it is to get hammers these days."

Mrs. Russell said, "Well, thank you anyway, Mrs. Quitrick," and hung up. She poured herself another cup of coffee and while she drank it she thought and thought about her little fighter-quarrelers. Then she had an idea. She would call Mrs. Piggle-Wiggle and ask her what to do.

Mrs. Piggle-Wiggle would know if anyone would.

She called Mrs. Piggle-Wiggle and said, "Mrs. Piggle-Wiggle, I am Mrs. Russell, the mother of Anne and Joan."

Mrs. Piggle-Wiggle said, "Oh, yes, the twins. Such darling little girls and so pretty."

Mrs. Russell said, "But they quarrel so, Mrs. Piggle-Wiggle. They begin fighting the moment they open their eyes in the morning and they don't stop until they fall asleep from exhaustion. It is dreadful, Mrs. Piggle-Wiggle. You should hear them!"

Mrs. Piggle-Wiggle said, "Oh, I know. 'That's my sock.' 'No, it's mine.' 'That's my box.' 'No, it's mine.' ' 'Tis not!' ' 'Tis too.' 'You have the most.' 'You're a pig!' "

Mrs. Russell said, "Why, Mrs. Piggle-Wiggle, you must have heard them. I was hoping they didn't quarrel when they were at your house."

Mrs. Piggle-Wiggle said, "No, I haven't heard Anne and Joan but I have heard hundreds of other children. You see Fighter-Quarreleritis is a common children's disease and it is very contagious, but very easy to cure."

"Easy to cure? Oh, Mrs. Piggle-Wiggle, how?" asked Mrs. Russell.

"Well," said Mrs. Piggle-Wiggle. "In the first place, fighting and quarreling are merely habits. One morning a child wakens and feels cross and so instead of smiling at his little brother and saying 'Good morning!' he glares at his little brother and shouts, 'You've got on MY shirt!' The little brother says, 'I have NOT!' because he hasn't. The cross child says, 'You have too. You have too!' and the quarreling has begun.

111

"The next morning both children have the Fighter-Quarreleritis and they wake and begin shouting rudely at each other. It soon becomes a habit and they forget how to be courteous.

"Now, Mrs. Russell, I believe that if Fighter-Quarrelers could hear themselves as others hear them and see themselves as others see them, they would soon realize how unpleasant they were and would be cured.

"In order to do this with Anne and Joan, you and Mr. Russell will have to pretend to be Anne and Joan. First, however, you must write down every single fighting thing that the children say. Begin with this morning and keep a careful record of the whole day. Say nothing to the twins but, tomorrow, you and Mr. Russell repeat their quarrels. I do not believe that it will be necessary to slap and pinch but be sure to be loud and noisy. Don't laugh and don't let the children know that it is just a game. Look quarrelsome as well as acting quarrelsome. One day usually is sufficient."

Mrs. Russell said, "Every morning Joan tells Anne that there is a big black spider in the bed on Anne's side and Anne comes screaming into our room. Should Mr. Russell and I do that?"

"My, my," said Mrs. Piggle-Wiggle. "That is the way Billy and Tommy Peters used to start the day, only Billy told Tommy it was a cobra. Well, cobra or black spider, you and Mr. Russell do the same. Goodbye and good luck!"

After saying goodbye to Mrs. Piggle-Wiggle, Mrs. Russell sat down and wrote down every word of Anne and Joan's morning quarreling that she could remember. After school she purposely gave one of them a bigger apple than she gave the other and then followed them around and wrote down the quarreling. She stayed in their room while they undressed for bed and took notes. Fortunately the children were very productive and fought about the amount of toothpaste on their toothbrushes, whose turn it was for the shower, whose pillow was softest, the amount of room they had in the bed, who had the most covers, whose turn it was to turn off the light, who had the biggest feet, whose mouth opened the widest, who had the most teeth, everything. My, they were naughty and disagreeable!

When she had finished writing it all down, Mrs. Russell handed a copy to Mr. Russell and told him about Mrs. Piggle-Wiggle. He thought it was a wonderful idea and studied his part carefully.

The next morning Joan opened her blue eyes and was just reaching out to pinch Anne when she heard a commotion in her mother's and daddy's room and suddenly the door flew open and in came Mrs. Russell clutching her bathrobe and squealing, "Anne, Joan, quick, there is a big black spider in our bed and it's on my side!"

Joan said calmly, "How do you know there's one? Did you see it?"

Anne awoke and out of habit she leapt out of bed and ran for the door squealing. Her mother squealed louder and

Anne, surprised, asked her what the trouble was. Her mother began pounding on the bed and yelling, "There's a big black spider in our bed on my side. Daddy said so. He saw it."

Anne said, "But, Mother, if there is a spider why is Daddy in there?"

Her mother paid no attention to her but continued to squeal, "Daddy said there was. I'm scared. Eeeeeeeeeee!"

Joan said, "We'd better go in and look, Anne." So they solemnly marched into their mother's and daddy's room. Mr. Russell was lying in bed gazing at the ceiling. Anne threw back the covers and Joan peered into the bed but all they could see were Daddy's feet, the toes wriggling.

Anne said sternly, "Why did you scare Mother that way, Daddy?"

Mr. Russell said, "Was she scared?" and jumped out of bed and ran into the bathroom shouting at the top of his voice, "Ha, ha, my first turn for the shower!"

At that Mrs. Russell came flying in from the twins' room and began pounding on the bathroom door, yelling, "It is not your first turn! It's mine! You traded me your first turn yesterday for a new golf ball."

Mr. Russell laughed rudely and called out, "Too bad for you. I've got the door locked."

Mrs. Russell kicked at the door and shouted, "Cheater, cheater, cheater!"

Anne and Joan looked at each other. Their eyes were

round with amazement. Anne whispered, "Let's get dressed," and Joan said, "Yes, let's hurry!" and they tiptoed out of the room, closing the door carefully behind them.

While they dressed they could hear their mother and father quarreling. When Mr. Russell came out of the shower, Mrs. Russell said, "You used my towel. That's my towel."

Mr. Russell said, " 'Tis not. It's mine."

Mrs. Russell said, " 'Tis not. It's mine."

Mr. Russell said, "That's MY shirt. You've got on my NEW T-Shirt."

Mrs. Russell said, "Well, you wore my golf sweater."

Mr. Russell said, "Take off MY NEW SHIRT!"

Mrs. Russell began to bawl. She sobbed, "You wore my golf sweater and you promised me that I could wear the shirt. You're a pig."

Mr. Russell said, "All right, baby, wear the old shirt."

At breakfast Mr. Russell took a little ruler out of his pocket and measured the grapefruit and then he took the biggest. Mother snatched it away from him and spilled coffee on the new T-shirt.

Mother served the scrambled eggs and gave herself a large heaping plate and Daddy a small serving. Daddy looked at both plates and said, "Pig!"

"Speaking of pigs," said Mrs. Russell, "it's my turn for the car!"

" 'Tis not," said Mr. Russell. "It's my turn. You had the car last week."

Mrs. Russell said, "I only drove up to the drugstore and back last week and you went clear out to the golf club."

Mr. Russell said in a very disagreeable way, "It makes no difference to me how far you drove, you have had your turn, madam."

Mrs. Russell began to bawl. "I think you're meeeeeeean," she wailed. "Isn't it my turn, girls?" she turned to the twins.

The girls looked at their mother but they didn't answer. Instead they asked to be excused, put on their coats and hurried off to school.

At dinner that night, Daddy took the chops up to the bathroom and weighed them on the scales and then took the two biggest. Mother took the biggest baked potato but she sorted the string beans out one by one so that everyone got an equal share but they were ice cold.

The twins cleared the table and Anne carried in the pumpkin pie. Now, pumpkin pie was the twins' very favorite dessert and so Anne was very careful to walk slowly and put the pie down gently in front of Daddy. But it was wasted effort for Mother reached over and grabbed the pie saying, "I'll SERVE THAT!"

"Oh, no, you won't," said Daddy jerking the pie back.

"Will too," said Mother reaching for the pie, but Daddy jerked it off the table and held it over his head. Mother grabbed his wrist and the pie went SPLAT all over the rug.

The twins began to cry. They said, "Mommy, Daddy, please stop quarreling. We just can't stand it any more. It's dreadful!"

Mother said, "Why, we thought you enjoyed fighting."

Joan said, "We hate quarreling. We are so unhappy!"

Anne said, "Fighting is terrible. It makes us miserable."

Mrs. Russell took Joan on her lap and Mr. Russell took Anne on his lap and they said, "To tell you the truth, girls, we don't like quarreling either. It is just a habit we caught from you. Why, we must have been quarreling all day."

The twins said, "You have, you have!"

Daddy said, "I'll tell you what we'll do. We'll all join hands and solemnly pledge that there shall be no more quarreling in this house. Then, we'll all walk up to Findley's Drugstore and seal the pledge with ice cream. Does everyone agree?"

"We all agree," they shouted. So they joined hands and said, "I do solemnly pledge that I will not quarrel or fight in this house ever again."

Then they walked up to Mr. Findley's drugstore and had ice cream sodas and even though Anne saw Mr. Findley put three scoops of ice cream in Joan's soda and only two in hers and even though Joan saw Mr. Findley put two scoops of strawberry in Anne's soda and only one in hers, they neither of them said a word. The Fighter-Quarreleritis was cured.

The End